Also by P. D. Ouspensky

Tertium Organum

A New Model of the Universe

Strange Life of Ivan Osokin

In Search of the Miraculous

The Psychology of Man's Possible Evolution

The Fourth Way

TALKS WITH A DEVIL

TALKS WITH A DEVIL

P. D. Ouspensky

Translated by Katya Petroff

Edited and with an Introduction by
J. G. Bennett

Alfred A. Knopf   *New York*   1973

THIS IS A BORZOI BOOK
PUBLISHED BY ALFRED A. KNOPF, INC.

Copyright © 1972 by Turnstone Press Ltd.

Library of Congress Cataloging in Publication Data

Uspenskiĭ, Petr Dem'ianovich, 1878-1947.
  Talks with a Devil.

  Translation of Razgovory s d'iavolom.
  I. Title.
PZ3.U88Ta13 [PG3476.U675]   891.7'3'44   73-4305
ISBN 0-394-48537-8

First published in Petrograd in 1916
under the title
РАЗГОВОРЫ СЪ ДЬЯВОЛОМЪ
Originally published in Great Britain
by Turnstone Press Ltd.,
London

Manufactured in the United States of America

FIRST AMERICAN EDITION

Contents

Introduction

In Holy Russia, devils and demons were very real participants in human life. Popular imagination saw the agency of nonhuman beings in every situation that could arise, in rivers, fields and forests, in the home and in the sky. The Slavs were descended from Asiatic hordes who for millennia had lived under the sway of magicians and shamans; after their conversion to Christianity, they retained many of their atavistic beliefs. A myth widely believed in Little Russia explained demons as descended from Adam and Eve, who had twelve pairs of children. Once when God was visiting them, Adam hid half his children because he had exceeded the quota of six pairs that God had prescribed for him. The twelve who did not receive God's blessing were the forebears of the race of demons who have ever since tormented mankind. It is also widely believed that Satan, the Evil One, was not God's creation but an independent power that had contributed to the creation of the world by making it subject to time and mortality. The Devil (*Diavol*) has his own huge retinue of subordinate devils whose task it is to circumvent the plans of God, the Good

Spirit. The devils are not hostile to man except insofar as man is the friend of God. It is they who have been responsible for every kind of technical progress: from them mankind learned the arts of ironworking, brewing, and distilling; the Devil himself discovered fire, built the first mill, and constructed the first wagon. The art of reading and writing was one of his great gifts to mankind. All these were bestowed to make man independent of God and so break the link whereby man was able to help God in governing the world. In this capacity the Devil is the "crafty one" (*Lukhavi*) who appears in the old Slavonic version of the Lord's Prayer in the words, "Deliver us from the crafty one."

There is an entirely different kind of devil called *Chort* who is more of a plague than a tempter. He is the ally of the witches and magicians who evoke the unclean spirits. Yet again, there are innumerable species of demons, sprites, fairies, and other nonhuman beings whose activities are even more pervasive than their Celtic counterparts. The most dreaded of these is Baba Yaga, a large and powerful female figure who plays a great part in Slavic legendary lore. The *Mora* or *Mara* who torment mankind are recognizable as *Mara* in Hindu and Buddhist legends of the temptations of Krishna and Gautama Buddha. The derivative *Kikamora* of the eastern Slavs becomes the presiding genius of forests and steppes. (An entire book could be written about all the varieties of nature spirits and their role in Slavic life.) There was also a household demon who if propitiated could be the friend of each family, but if crossed could bring every kind of misfortune. All illnesses and misfortunes were ascribed to demons, each of which had dominion over a particular disease.

This brief sketch should suffice to show why Ouspensky,

brought up in the forests, of relatively humble but ancient stock, would find it natural to take a devil as the hero of his tale, as Gurdjieff was to do later in *Beelzebub's Tales to His Grandson*. There is, however, a decisive difference inasmuch as Beelzebub is depicted as an extraterrestrial being, whereas Ouspensky's devils are truly Slavic in their obsession with the material world. The influence of Manicheanism, which penetrated into Russia in the second century A.D., can be seen in Ouspensky's fanatical hatred of materialism as he saw it exemplified in Marxism and the Russian Revolution.

Ouspensky used to tell us that in his family the names Peter and Damien had passed from father to son alternately for many generations. The tradition had it that the Damiens were ascetic world-haters and the Peters joyful lovers of life. He said that both characteristics had entered into him. He was indeed a man with two opposing natures, and this dualism colored his life and his writings. I first met him in 1920, soon after he arrived in Constantinople from the Caucasus with his wife Sophie Grigorevna, her daughter, and her one-year-old son, Leonidas, known to us all as Lonya. The city was overcrowded with repatriated Turkish soldiers, with the Allied Army of Occupation, and tens of thousands of Russian refugees. Ouspensky found a room for his family on Biyuk Ada—that is, Prinkipo to the Levantines, and L'Ile des Princes to foreigners. They had brought very few possessions out of Russia, and Ouspensky had to find a way of supporting himself and his family by teaching English, which he himself spoke with difficulty, to Russians who hoped to go to England to await the collapse of the Revolution which they confidently expected. Nearly all the Russians I met at that time were making plans for their return to Russia. Ouspensky had no such illusions and feared, on the contrary, that Bolshevism would spread through Germany and from Germany all over Europe. He thought that England might escape the coming revolution by allying herself firmly with the United States.

Another Russian who knew that Tsarist Russia and perhaps even "Holy Russia" had gone forever was Alexander Lvov, a former colonel of the Imperial Horse Guard and a member of the highest Russian aristocracy, who had given up lands and title to follow Tolstoy. He was able to support himself by the trade of shoemaking, which he had learned in order to become one of the proletariat. In 1920 Lvov was staying with Mrs. Beaumont, who was later to become my wife, in her flat in a large timber-built apartment house near the German Embassy. One day Lvov asked if a friend could use her drawing room for meetings of an occult group. The leader of this group was Ouspensky, who began to come regularly every Wednesday from Prinkipo to conduct meetings of some twenty to thirty Russians. He and I soon became friends and he began to tell me about the remarkable "System" in which he was interested. About the same time, but in quite different circumstances, I met Gurdjieff, the author of the "System," and several of his pupils who had come with him from Tiflis.

In 1921, Ouspensky showed me an English translation of his book *Tertium Organum* which he had just received from Nicky Bessarabov. A cable had come from Lady Rothermere, who was then in New York, inviting him to meet her in England. At that time there was a general instruction to British consuls to curtail visas to émigré Russians, but I was able to convince the British Consulate that Ouspensky was a highly desirable visitor and procured visas for him and his family. When I returned to London in 1922, I joined the group led by Orage and Maurice Nicoll to which Ouspensky was unveiling the remarkable corpus of psychological, cosmological, and historical ideas that constituted Gurdjieff's "System" and was also introducing his techniques of self-development.

As soon as I settled in London in 1922, I became an active member of Ouspensky's circle. I used to meet him privately at his flat in Gwendwr Road in West Kensington nearly every week. We would work together on the translation of his books from the Russian. He was very ready to talk about his early life and the experiences that had led him to believe that our usual views about time, matter, and existence itself were all illusory. These talks were often continued halfway through the night at a Chinese restaurant in Oxford Street that he found particularly congenial. He was a connoisseur of exotic foods from many countries and had such a fine taste in China tea that he became one of the select group that Twinings in the Strand used every year to invite to give their opinion of the new tea crop.

In his conversations Ouspensky betrayed the deep conflict between his belief in law and order, his hatred of the Bolsheviks, and his contempt for the illiterate masses that came from one side of his nature, and his recognition that all people, whether rulers or ruled, are equally helpless to change or to do anything as they intend. His personal rejection of materialism, which shows itself in *Talks with a Devil,* comes from an attitude towards life very different from Gurdjieff's rejection of human pretensions in his doctrine of man as a machine with almost no power to do anything. At that time Ouspensky was working on the notes he had made during the period from 1915 to 1918, during which he had been a pupil of Gurdjieff, first in Russia and then in the Caucasus. He had at that time no intention of publishing this material, but suggested that it could be read aloud at group meetings. At that time increasing numbers of people in London were becoming interested in Ouspensky's meetings, and he had no time to meet all the groups himself. He therefore delegated to me and to others the task of reading from his books and to some extent explaining their content.

In 1922 Ouspensky worked hard to help Gurdjieff in launching his Institute for the Harmonious Development of Man at the Prieuré in Fontainebleau. At first we all hoped that this might be in London, but the British Foreign Office was adamant in advising the Home Office to refuse residential permits to Gurdjieff and his group. I was well aware that the government in India regarded Gurdjieff as a Russian agent very hostile to Britain, and concluded that the dossier I had seen in Turkey had followed him to England and was the main obstacle to his receiving permission to settle in this country. It seems to me that this hostility to Gurdjieff in those early days remained to the end of his life and accounted for the fact that he never again came to England.

Ouspensky's personal position was extremely sensitive, and it says much for his loyalty to Gurdjieff that he persisted in trying to arrange for the necessary permits. It was not until two years later, in the spring of 1924, that Ouspensky completely changed his attitude and advised all his own pupils to have nothing more to do with Gurdjieff. According to Boris Mouravieff, who had known Ouspensky in Russia and had first met Gurdjieff in Turkey in 1921, Ouspensky turned away from Gurdjieff on moral grounds. In an unpublished study of Ouspensky and Gurdjieff, Mouravieff describes a visit to Paris immediately after Gurdjieff's nearly fatal accident in 1921 and recalls Ouspensky's outburst: "If someone close to you, your near relative, turned out to be a criminal, what would you do?" Such attitudes exemplify the ascetic, puritanical side of Ouspensky's nature, which was an insurmountable obstacle to his understanding of Gurdjieff, who was not concerned with differences between people—materialist or spiritualist, brutish or cultured, evil or good—but with the objective significance of human life, or as he himself put it, "the sense and purpose of human existence on the earth."

The difference stands out if we compare the books written by Ouspensky before and after this meeting with Gurdjieff in 1915. Ouspensky's reputation, particularly in pre-1914 Russia and post-1945 U.S.A., rests mainly on his remarkable *Tertium Organum,* the central theme of which is the need to go beyond logical thinking if we are to understand the nature of the real world. Western readers know Ouspensky mainly through this book and through his *In Search of the Miraculous.* The first is entirely his own and the second is almost entirely Gurdjieff. Between them comes *A New Model of the Universe,* which is to a considerable extent influenced by his travels between 1908 and 1915. Little is known of this period of his life, and I can report only the episodes that I heard from him in the course of conversations. He was a successful journalist, sometimes working for the leading Russian papers, but more often as a free lance. He traveled in Europe and the United States, writing articles for St. Petersburg papers, between 1908 and 1912. The first story in the present book, "The Inventor," shows his knowledge of New York at the time that Theodore Roosevelt was President of the U.S.A. He had never been to the West Coast and told me that he regretted this, though not so much as his inability to visit Japan. In 1912 he achieved his ambition to go to India with an open commission to write articles for three Russian papers. He met some of the outstanding yogis of the time, including Aurobindo, who was already established in Pondicherry. He was not impressed by any of them. He explained afterwards that he was looking for "real knowledge" and found only holy men who may have achieved liberation for themselves but could not transmit their methods to others. He also spent some time at Adhyar in Madras, the headquarters of the Theosophical Society. In later years he liked to tell the story of the "caste system" at Adhyar. On the ground floor were all the hangers-on and undistinguished visitors. The second floor was reserved for well-wishers who gave their money and support to the society. The top floor with a large open roof was the home of the esoteric group, the real initiates of Theosophy. Ouspensky recalled with relish that he was at once admitted to the esoteric group in spite of his not being a member of the Theosophical Society and his open criticism of their founder, Helena Blavatsky. He asserted that he found nothing at Adhyar that made him wish to stay.

He went on to Ceylon, which he found more congenial, and he met several of the more famous *bhikku*'s and satisfied himself that the old techniques of Buddhism were still being practiced in Ceylon. But once again he felt no urge to cut himself off from the West and become a monk. He wrote later that he was not interested in a way that would isolate him from the Western world, which held the key to the future of mankind. This did not mean that he doubted the existence of "schools," as he called them, in India and Ceylon, but that these schools no longer had the significance that they used to have in the past. He also added that he had found that most of these schools relied upon religious and devotional techniques that he was convinced were insufficient for penetrating into the essential reality for which he was seeking.

When Ouspensky returned to Russia, the whole course of his life was changed by his meeting with Gurdjieff. Gurdjieff's system for the Harmonious Development of Man offered so many possibilities that are not to be found in either the Buddhist scriptures, the *Nikayas,* or in the methods of the Theravadins of the present time, that Ouspensky found a new hope. The present book was written before this meeting, and unlike his later writings was not revised in the light of what he learned from Gurdjieff. It can be put in a bracket with *Tertium Organum* and *Ivan*

Osokin as "pure Ouspensky." *Ivan Osokin* was admittedly largely autobiographical, and from it we can discern the features of Ouspensky's life at school. It was first published in Russia as *Cinemadrama* to express Ouspensky's insights into eternal recurrence, but I believe that he changed the ending after meeting Gurdjieff, who himself was brought in as the magician (to represent the "Work" as Ouspensky conceived it) who shows Osokin the way to escape from the cycle of recurrent failure ending in suicide, in which he had been trapped.

Ouspensky's concept of human destiny was clearly bound up with the idea of "escape." In later years this need to escape from recurrence became almost an obsession, which he transmitted to his closest followers, such as Rodney Collin Smith and Dr. Francis Roles. Avoidance of involvement in the world process was associated with the idea of escaping from recurrence. Like many other Russians he dreamed of a cultured spirituality which would create an environment in which an enlightened few could withdraw from the world and privately achieve liberation. This dream never entirely left him.

Ouspensky was, however, entirely unable to follow Gurdjieff through the final stages of his work. The reasons for this are not relevant to the present book, but the outcome was that after giving Gurdjieff his full support up to the time of his going to America in 1923, he entirely changed in 1924 while Gurdjieff was still in America. From that time until the end of his life, he had no direct communication with Gurdjieff, though he remained passionately interested in everything Gurdjieff was doing.

After his break with Gurdjieff, Ouspensky returned to his earlier writings and made a compilation which he published in 1929 with the title *A New Model of the Universe*. At that time my own relations with him were very close. We were both very much interested in the nature of time and eternity, and believed that important discoveries in this field would attract attention to the "System" which Ouspensky ascribed to a school of wisdom from which we could still hope to get the help we needed, without having to pass through Gurdjieff, whom he regarded as a "tainted channel." *A New Model of the Universe* is a series of loosely connected essays with a common theme that the current conceptions of man and the universe were profoundly misleading and would have to be discarded. At one time he thought of including one of the *Talks with a Devil* —I think it was "The Benevolent Devil"—in *A New Model of the Universe.* He finally decided to omit the story as being out of keeping with the philosophical character of the book. (Most of the material had been written before 1914 and had been published in Russian newspapers for which Ouspensky had worked as a journalist.) At this time Ouspensky was still writing in Russian, and he sent one copy of the Russian text to Paris to be translated into French by the Baroness Rausch, while another copy was translated into English by Mrs. Kent, herself of a noble Russian family, and other Russians in his own circle. I helped with the translation, particularly in making sure that Ouspensky's meaning was correctly interpreted.

It was at this time that Ouspensky first spoke to me about his *Talks with a Devil.* He told me that these two stories had been written to express his belief that man's chief error is to believe that the material world is the only reality. This belief, he said, is the source of most human troubles because people fight uselessly over unreal issues, disregarding the real problem, which is that of liberation from our attachment to matter. *Talks with a Devil* had been written while Ouspensky was in India and Ceylon in 1914 and had been published with a new ending in a

St. Petersburg newspaper in the early days of the war. The edition from which the present translation is made was published in Petrograd in 1916. All Ouspensky's copies were lost with the rest of his library after the October Revolution in Moscow. He had sent a few copies to friends abroad and suggested that I might be able to trace them through the Theosophical Society. Miss Maud Hoffman, a leading theosophist and a friend of Leadbeater and Mrs. Besant, discovered that a copy had reached the British Museum Library. I found it under the name of Uspenski, P. D., and was able to obtain two photographed copies, one of which Ouspensky invited me to retain with a view to possible translation.

Talks with a Devil clearly belongs to Ouspensky's *Wanderjahren,* when he was searching for the secret which he believed to be hidden in the schools of India and Ceylon. His theosophical leanings are demonstrated by his unwillingness to look to the Levant or even to Central Asia for the source of teaching. Though disappointed with the Theosophical Society as he found it at Adhyar, he accepted much of their philosophy. He was particularly fascinated by the theosophical cycle of historical recurrence. He often referred to this in later years and talked of the world wars as evidence that we were entering the last stages of the Dark Cycle. This theme evidently colors his treatment of "The Benevolent Devil."

It is interesting to remember that Ouspensky was a great admirer of Robert Louis Stevenson and said that he had been influenced by the fable called "The King of Duntrine's Daughter," which expresses the same theme of eternal recurrence with hints at the secret of freedom. He coupled Stevenson with Nietzsche as the two men from whom he had learned most about recurrence in his early years.

Talks with a Devil does not adequately express the agony of indecision through which Ouspensky lived in the later years of his life. This may be one reason for his not publishing it. I think also that in some way he associated it with his youthful illusion that spirituality and humanism could go hand in hand if only religion could be eliminated from the one and materialism from the other. He did once tell me that he had notes for a third talk that would pull the whole thing together. I think he had in mind to show the role of the "Work" as a third force that can reconcile spirit and matter, but could not find a way to make this theme sufficiently dramatic. Shortly before the outbreak of the Second World War, he told some of his pupils that he saw little hope of finding the source of the teaching he had been imparting. Something was missing and without new knowledge we should have to be reconciled to finding our own way of liberation. In the last weeks of his life, in 1947, he publicly repudiated the "System" as he had received it from Gurdjieff and called upon his followers to make a fresh start each in his or her own way.

The two stories published in this book examine two problems that for Ouspensky were very serious and important. The first is that of "conscious evil." He was well aware of the Eastern doctrines which on the whole deny the possibility of an evil will and treat evil as the absence of good or at worst the consequences of attachment to the external world. He had also from his childhood been exposed to the doctrine of original sin, which he could neither accept nor reject. Once he set his groups in London the task of trying to perform an act of conscious evil. We were all astonished by our inability to do a single evil act intentionally while fully aware that we were constantly doing far worse things and even knowing that we were doing them. Ouspensky insisted that evil is sleep, mechanicalness, and the absence of intention, for which we are indirectly responsible because it is in our power not to be asleep and mechanical, but which we cannot directly control. This theme runs through the story of the inventor, who does harm particularly when he intends to do good, and cannot bring himself to accept the disastrous consequences of his own work of genius. He realizes that he had never asked himself what would happen if his brainchild were to prove an overwhelming success. In this, the story of the inventor is evidently an allegory of modern man faced with the consequences of the miracles of science and technology.

He carries the story forward in a very telling way by showing that the inventor, always in control of the material forces, begins to invest them with a new quality, a quality that alienates him from the Devil and finally leads to the disappearance of the Devil, who can no longer understand or follow him in his high search for a beneficent use of the material forces that he had unleased. All that is left of the Devil is a smell of sulfur.

On the very first page, Ouspensky hints at the deeper significance in the story. The Devil, "strictly speaking," does not exist: he and his crew are only what man makes them. The Devil can do no more than suggest, and even his suggestion turns out to be the autosuggestion of man himself. Man infects the material world with a diabolical character that is not inherent, but he is also able to become aware of the reality of other values. So the Devil in the story is constantly inveighing against the artists and the mystics that are aware of some other world than the world of matter; and this other world is one in which the diabolical suggestions have no place.

Ouspensky is and remains a dualist because he sees the diabolical values as those man imputes to the material, quantity-ridden world, but he distinguishes these false, diabolical values from those of artistic appreciation, of religious experience and spiritual quality. Ouspensky himself recalls that when he met Gurdjieff, he tried to insist upon this distinction but Gurdjieff brushed it aside, saying, "All are mechanical. It is no matter whether the values are spiritual or materialistic. What matters is whether they are mechanical or conscious."

This was clearly a novel idea for Ouspensky, and one which he had not appreciated at the time that he wrote "The Inventor" or "The Benevolent Devil" which follows it. Nevertheless, Ouspensky does produce the concept of matter as a mode of being. He uses the term GREAT MATTER (the capital letters are in the Russian text) to indicate that he is not talking about matter in terms of its vast scale in the universe, quantitative immensity, but its status as a mode of existence. In this sense, Ouspensky was certainly a dualist, seeing the Great Matter as the resistance to the creative power of God. Ouspensky's most inspired work, *Tertium Organum,* is devoted to the thesis—almost a revelation—that logical thinking imprisons man in the material world. The "third instrument" which he claims to have discovered is the creative insight that goes beyond logic. This notion colors all Ouspensky's writing and is seen in the Devil's abhorrence of artists and mystics who cannot think logically and normally. Matter and logic are the substance of diabolical suggestion.

Gurdjieff, on the other hand, looked upon matter and energy as interchangeable (this, long before Einstein's equations had been understood), and he also taught that the level of materiality is correlative to the level of Consciousness or the level of Being. These were startling ideas for Ouspensky when he first heard them in 1915, and he did not attempt to embody them in his revision of "The Inventor."

"The Inventor" was written for publication in a Russian periodical, and no doubt Ouspensky had in mind a readership which called for both sentimental and sensational material. The episodes connected with the invention and the subsequent explosion of interest due to its use in particularly dramatic circumstances are somewhat repetitive and at times tedious. I have, therefore, taken it upon myself to shorten some of these episodes and to cut out some of the purely narrative part of the story. I have left everything that is relevant to the theme that Ouspensky wishes to convey and which undoubtedly for him was the real purpose of the two stories. I have done this because Ouspensky himself was quite ruthless in cutting his own material when he used his old Russian publications for putting together his book *The New Model of the Universe.*

When we turn to "The Benevolent Devil," the story becomes much more vivid because it is largely based upon Ouspensky's own travels in India and Ceylon, and he was able to give a firsthand account of the caves of Alhora which he visited in 1913 and also the Buddhist temples which he went to in Ceylon.

The devil (in this tale Ouspensky did not capitalize the word, indicating the plurality of the demonhood) is presented as seeking to prevent us from waking up to the situation, which is that we are imprisoned in materiality only because we will not face and accept the truth that reality is not of this world. The suggestion that runs through both these stories, that devils are interested in man only when he makes a real effort to escape, represents a viewpoint to which Ouspensky often returned. There is a law that every positive striving must inevitably arouse an equally strong negative reaction. Although this is exemplified again and again in the history of mankind—on the small scale no less than upon the large one—we do not wish to face it.

Only a few people can recognize that the price of doing the right thing is inevitably to expose oneself to opposition and even to the threat of destruction; these men are different from ordinary men and would recognize one another but for the devil's precautions to prevent it.

The Benevolent Devil desires mankind to be happy and not concern itself with the pursuit of a chimerical "other world." Here we recognize the theme of Gurdjieff's *"organ kundabuffer"* of which Ouspensky had certainly heard nothing when the story was written. "The Benevolent Devil" emphasizes the significance of man's delusion and self-deception. Man remains earthbound because he is asleep to reality and does not wish to awaken. He conceives "good" in terms of the illusory world, where in any case, nothing can be accomplished. The devil's task is to encourage this deception, and he does so with well-meaning people by playing on the illusion that well-meaning and well-doing are one and the same. "Nobility" is the trump card by which he wins the final battle.

In "The Benevolent Devil," Ouspensky clearly borrows from the Slavic legend of the division of mankind into the accepted and the rejected children of Adam. He modifies the legend to make the descendants of Adam capable of perceiving Reality, while those who are descended from the animals are cut off. It is only the descendants of Adam who have the possibility of waking up and acquiring a "soul."

Ouspensky could not make up his mind about the unfairness of life which opens such great opportunities to the few and seems to deny hope to the many. He was experimenting in this story with an account of evil that goes back to Zoroastrian origins. In the *Avesta,* the races of men and animals are descended from the man Gayomart and from the bull Gösh Urvan. The *Avesta* do not label these good and evil, but rather assign them different roles in the struggle between the good and evil spirits. These traditions reached the Slav people before their migrations to the West, and, being divorced from their religions and cosmological origins, turned into fairy stories and folklore. Ouspensky could recognize something of the original significance and was able to use them to convey his own message.

Man is vulnerable on both sides of his nature—that which strives towards the light no less than that which seeks the darkness. The diabolical suggestion that plays on man's nobility can bring about a greater downfall than the temptations that beset his animal nature. Ouspensky was aware that "evil" forces were working to destroy human freedom and could see that these forces could not be overcome in a direct confrontation because the "good" forces were divided among themselves by such slogans as "patriotism," "self-sacrifice," and "devotion to a cause"— all of which can be exploited by the devil.

In these stories, the devil fails to achieve his objectives no less helplessly than his would-be victims. The world is thoroughly irrational, and we must not expect to find answers to our questions or morals to our stories. This seems to be the message that Ouspensky wishes to convey. His pessimism was temporarily lifted by his contact with Gurdjieff, but it descended upon him again when he saw that Gurdjieff was not the man he had pictured and hoped for.

I recall vividly a winter evening in 1924 when I was with Ouspensky at Gwendwr Road. He stood in front of the gas fire in the dingy sitting room and as if speaking to himself said: "We cannot know if this work is possible, but we do know that without it there is no hope. We must not give up even if we do not see any evidence that it will lead us out of the darkness. There is nothing else and this one certainty we must hold onto." Since then forty-eight

years have passed, and I have become convinced not only
that there is nothing else, but also that man is not in a
hopeless predicament. We are in a serious crisis—more
serious even than Ouspensky foresaw—and we are hypnotized by material forces. The very gravity of the crisis is
bringing about an awakening. Man is beginning to see the
threat to his very existence, and there are many who are
prepared to accept the challenge that Leslie White could
not understand.

Ouspensky's intuitive grasp that some people can see
reality when the majority can see only the appearance is
even more relevant today than when he wrote this story
sixty years ago. If enough people can be brought to see and
accept the challenge, mankind will make a great step forward. But it also seems the case that there are cunning
forces at work whose aim is to prevent the awakening of
those who have the possibility of seeing. Ouspensky's allegory of the devil is too near the truth to be comfortable.

It is a source of real satisfaction to have been able to
contribute to the preservation of one part of Ouspensky's
literary work. Miss Ekaterina Petroff worked intermittently
with me for several years in making the translation. Miss
Anna Durkova helped in editing and with her knowledge
of Slavic folklore. I hope that the result will commend itself to old admirers of Ouspensky no less than to new
readers.

JOHN G. BENNETT
Sherborne, Gloucestershire

June, 1972

THE
INVENTOR

I will tell you a fairy tale," said the Devil, "on one condition: you must not ask me the moral. You may draw any conclusion you like, but please do not question me. As it is, far too many follies are laid at our door, yet we, strictly speaking, do not even exist. It is you who create us."

My story takes place in New York some twenty-five years ago. There lived then a young man by the name of Hugh B.; I will not tell you his full name, but you will soon guess it for yourself. His name is known now to people in all five parts of the globe. But then he was completely unknown.

I will start at a tragic moment in the life of this young man, when he was traveling from one of the suburbs of New York to Manhattan, with the intention of buying a revolver and then shooting himself on a lonely shore on Long Island; in a spot which had remained in his memory from the times of boyhood excursions, when he and his playmates, pretending to be explorers, had discovered unknown countries around New York.

His intention was very definite and the decision final. All in all, it was a very common occurrence in the life of a big city, something encountered repeatedly; in fact, to be frank, I have had to arrange similar events thousands and tens of thousands of times. However, this time such a common beginning had a quite uncommon sequel and a most uncommon result.

Nevertheless before turning to the outcome of the day, I must tell you in detail all that led up to it.

Hugh was a born inventor. From early childhood, when walking with his mother in the park or playing with other children, or simply sitting quietly in a corner building with bricks or drawing monsters, he invented incessantly, constructing in his mind a variety of extraordinary contrivances, improvements for everything in the world.

He derived a special satisfaction from inventing improvements and adaptations for his aunt. He would draw her with a chimney, or on wheels. For one drawing, in which this not-young maiden was portrayed with six legs and other variations, little Hugh was severely punished. It was one of his first memories.

Not long after this, Hugh learned first to design and then to make models of his inventions. By this time he had learned that live people cannot be improved upon. Nevertheless his inventions were, of course, all pure fantasy; when he was fourteen, he nearly drowned himself trying out homemade water skis of his own design.

At the time my story begins, he was about twenty-six years old. He had been married for several years and worked as a draftsman in a large engineering factory; he lived in an apartment of three minute rooms, the size of ship's cabins, in an enormous and ugly brick building in one of the suburbs of New York. He was very dissatisfied with his life.

The slaves who toil in our offices and factories are invariably barely conscious of their enslavement. If they have any dreams they are merely of ways of improving their slavery: having a good time on a Sunday; going to a dance in the evening; dressing up like a gentleman; and getting more money. Even if they are dissatisfied with their life, they think only of shortening the hours of work, or increasing their salaries and holidays—in a nutshell, all the trappings of the Socialist Utopia. They could never, even mentally, bring themselves to revolt against work itself. It is their God, and they do not dare oppose him even in thought. But Hugh was made of other stuff. He hated slavery. He always said that being a slave to work was the wrath of God. The very fibers of his being stirred with an awareness of this octopus, penetrating him with its tightening stranglehold. Quite apart from this, the thought of embellishing his slavery would never have occurred to him, nor was he the sort to delude himself with cheap distractions.

His mother died when he was sixteen, and he was forced to leave school and become an apprentice in the drawing office of a factory at a salary of five dollars a week.

This was the beginning of his career. Outwardly he differed little from the other apprentices in the drawing office. He copied drawings of machines, prepared paper and colors, sharpened pencils, and ran errands among the various departments of the factory. But at heart he did not for a moment accept this life.

Hugh's background was different from that of the majority of those surrounding him, and it played an important part in forming his attitudes. His companions were the children of toil and want, sons of factory workers like themselves and recent immigrants come to America to escape from hunger and cold and the greed of landlords, and from unemployment. Their world was small, limited, narrow, and dominated by the ever-present struggle against hunger and want. Quite different voices spoke within Hugh. He belonged to an old American family, descended from pioneers who had seen the virgin forest land of big lakes and rivers and who had fought the Indians. Among his ancestors were members of Congress, generals in the War of Independence, and rich plantation owners of the Southern States.

His father had lost the last of the family fortune during the Civil War, in which he had fought as an officer in the army of the South. He had been wounded and taken prisoner, but had escaped to Canada, where he married a young French-Canadian girl, and died a few years later. During his childhood, Hugh's mother had told him of her own sea-captain ancestors and of his father's—of the splendor of life on the plantations which she herself had never seen; of Hugh's great-grandfather, who had been Governor of South Carolina; of the Mexican War; of expeditions to the Far West. Hugh grew up with these tales, and they constituted a part of his being. It was hardly surprising, therefore, that the style of life conceived by his fellow workers should be too narrow for him. In truth, from the bottom of his heart he despised the factory workers and factory life with all that it could give him.

The factory itself, however, and the machines in it interested him deeply. He would spend hours in front of some machine, trying to understand it, to get to the heart of it. He collected the various catalogues and price lists which gave descriptions of machines; studied diagrams, drawings, photographs; spent whole nights with books on mechanics and mechanical engineering, whatever he could lay his hands on. And all the time new combinations of valves, wheels, levers—new inventions, each more amazing than the last—floated through his head.

Not for a second, though, did he stop hating and resenting his slavery. Often at night, when the need to get up at six in the morning forced him to abandon his precious books for sleep, he would make grim resolutions, swearing he would rather die than surrender to the fate of such a life. He was not deluding himself and was well aware of the obstacles which stood in his way. To escape his bondage it was necessary to snatch time away from it, yet always the iron hand of compulsory labor pressed on his shoulder. Now and then this need let up for a few hours (on rare occasions for several days) only to clamp down on him more strongly later. Hugh resented this, and fought for every hour.

Nonetheless, to look at he was a cheerful, lively, and high-spirited young American. The difference was that he was unable *not to think*. In this he was distinguished from the others.

During his first two years in the factory Hugh came to realize the gravity of his position; at first he was not unduly worried, for he had great faith in himself, his powers, and his future inventions, but later on he began to notice that he was beginning to give in to the factory's way of life involuntarily; this life and its people had already impressed him with their stamp. From that time on, his disgust and hatred of this enslavement were increased by his dread of facing it.

After four years of service in the factory something happened which brought about an immediate change in his position. He had been given some smudged diagrams of a new machine to redraw. While making the copy, Hugh found a mistake in the calculations. At the same time a strikingly simple and practical improvement, which nearly doubled the output of the machine, also occurred to him. He took his report to the engineer who had designed the machine. The engineer, not wishing to admit his error, started shouting and turned Hugh out. Hugh then went to the Director, who at first received him grimly; but in the end, when he had understood what Hugh was proposing, the Director saw that he was right.

At once everything changed. Hugh got a bonus for the improvement he had devised and he was given the post of senior draftsman. Instead of copying, he was entrusted with working out diagrams from sketches made by engineers. People began to consult him, and the Director who discovered him predicted that he would go far.

Of all the factory workers, it was on Hugh that this unexpected success had the least impact. He accepted everything as his due. He told himself that destiny must give him all he dreamed of, and achievement at the factory was so trivial in comparison with his dreams that it was not even worthy of serious discussion. But, of course, his conditions improved. He rented a small apartment, set up a workshop where he worked on his inventions in the evenings and on Sundays. He started with the idea of a pocket motor for hand-held instruments, but this device did not turn out to be very practical. Then he invented a guided torpedo, then an automatic brake for hoisting gear, then it was a great variety of things. But he was hampered by a lack of theoretical grounding and the time-consuming demands of the factory. However, to leave the factory seemed impossible—the more so now, for soon after his promotion Hugh had married Madge O'Neill. He was then twenty-two years old.

It had come about quite spontaneously—as something happens which had to happen. One Sunday Hugh had gone to the zoo in Central Park. He had long wanted to have a look at the big birds, especially the condors. (At that time he was working on an aircraft.) There, by the fence in front of the condors, stood a tall, cheerful, black-haired and black-eyed girl in a large red hat. She was chatting with a girl with an Irish accent, and several times, laughing, she glanced at Hugh. Not knowing how, Hugh got into conversation with her. Together they left the condors and before they knew it they had walked around the whole zoo. Hugh had not intended to look at bison and monkeys, but for some reason he enjoyed himself enormously. Hugh learned that Madge worked as a translator and stenographer in the office of a German company, that her parents were dead, that she had a small brother, and that the following Sunday she would be going to the shore with her friend. They met the following Sunday. Then they began to meet in the evenings. Eventually Hugh came to feel that he needed Madge as much as his inventions.

They decided to marry, and Hugh was convinced that no woman in the world was more beautiful and clever than Madge. He felt extremely happy and did not doubt that now he would succeed.

During one of their walks, discussing their future married life, Hugh said that they must not have children so long as their circumstances remained the same; in other words, so long as his inventions were not a real source of income, leaving him free of work and able to enjoy an affluent and easy life.

Madge was pleased when he started to speak like this, pleased with the talk itself, that is. It was daring—so she told herself. She was pleasantly excited when they talked about the children they would or would not have. She agreed with Hugh, pretending that she understood. Her only reservation was that Hugh had not said more, but had changed the subject, and had not explained how they would contrive not to have children. At that moment the idea seemed to Madge to be thrillingly improper. She could not have known, then, that their decision would bring her suffering and would be the cause of dissension between them, and have many other consequences.

Hugh was a delight to Madge then. She liked to hear him talk about his future inventions which would bring them millions; about his ancestors in South Carolina and the glittering life they led. But sometimes she wanted to laugh during these episodes, for Hugh got carried away and talked as though he had himself attended their festivities, and as though he had already become a rich and famous inventor. Madge nevertheless believed in him. But later, the dreams of Hugh and Madge went in different directions. Hugh's fantasies knew no bounds: a villa in Sorrento, a castle in Venice, his own yacht, travels in India and Japan, acquaintance with all the world's celebrities, with writers and artists; the capitals of the world at his feet. More inventions would follow, each more amazing than the last, completely revolutionizing the whole of life on earth and bringing them countless millions.

Listening to Hugh musing in this way, Madge seemed to hear the voice of her little brother, whose ambition was to fight Red Indians when he grew up. Madge began to think that men were only overgrown children and should be treated accordingly. A villa in Sorrento and hunting a scalp sounded pretty much the same to Madge.

Madge's own dreams were more realistic and mundane. Like any woman, she dreamed of finery, of hats and frocks; but characteristically she could not think in the abstract. She longed only for a dress or a hat she had glimpsed in a shop window. Lack of imagination, perhaps? Still, she had some fine dreams—she thought, for example, that it would be delightful to go to town and spend in one day a hundred or even two hundred dollars on whatever she fancied. Then she longed for a nice apartment, or a house with new furniture straight from the store; or for a trip to a seaside resort, or better still, somewhere "in the mountains," which sounded more aristocratic. She dreamed, too, of going to the theater, to the opera and concerts as often as she liked; of sitting in a box or the front row and listening to famous singers, seeing all around her the most prominent men and women, whose names she knew from the newspapers. The gossip columnists' accounts of the life of high society, and, in particular, the thinly veiled allusions to its scandals, constituted the favorite reading matter of the girls in the office where she worked.

But Madge was not completely vulgar; indeed, she was superior to most of her friends: she read books such as Bellamy's *Looking Backward* and *In a Hundred Years,* which gave descriptions of the ideal socialist state; and she was very enthusiastic about the "simple life," the "return to nature," and so on. More than anything in the world she loved flowers and children, and truly, her dreams lay in that quarter, though to herself this was not at all clear. She wanted very much to believe that she loved Hugh; that she was in sympathy with him and had faith in his inventions.

So they married, and lived in the small apartment in the huge house for nearly five years.

These five years held little reward for Hugh. His inventions had had no practical result, and the work in the factory depressed him more and more. At first, after his quick promotion and the improvement in his financial situation, he seemed satisfied. But meeting Madge, and his marriage, made him yearn for freedom again with renewed intensity.

Hugh loved Madge very much and longed to be with her all the time. But in fact, he hardly ever saw her. He spent the day in the office and the evenings in his workshop. Every so often he would tear himself away from the workshop and, with aching heart, take Madge out for the evening. But he felt that in doing this he was wronging her, for it merely postponed the hour of their liberation. This spoiled his pleasure, and then, in the morning, he had once again to suffer the office tearing him away.

All this was unusually painful to Hugh, because he had visions of spending days at a time with Madge, of reading with her, and traveling to the far corners of Europe and the East to see all the wonders he dreamed about unceasingly. Both his liberation and the realization of his dreams were to be achieved through his inventions, but the way was forever barred by the job which exhausted him, took up all his time, and interfered with his real work.

Hugh became convinced that the factory was taking liberties with his talent for invention. The improvement he had devised, for which he had received a bonus of five hundred dollars and the increased salary which seemed huge but was actually miserable and considerably smaller than the salary of his predecessor, had probably earned the factory hundreds of thousands of dollars. The device, which bore the trademark of the firm, was now used on all machine-tool benches made by the factory and was their characteristic feature. Many inventions followed upon this one, but Hugh was never again awarded a bonus. Inventions came to be expected of him. He was presented with a particular problem and a demand for its solution. The factory was obviously exploiting him. Hugh could see and feel this forced labor, draining his imagination and hindering his own projects and ideas.

So he decided to give less of himself to the factory. He

was hurt that his gifts were not valued. Inwardly he seethed with indignation. "I could do a great deal for them," he would say to himself, "if they were capable of valuing my work and paying for it."

Hugh knew well that an old type of factory boss who knew his business through and through, who understood and loved it and knew his employees, would have treated Hugh carefully. He would have seen that Hugh's talent for invention represented capital and would have made him a shareholder in the business, with a share in the profits of his inventions.

Hugh's factory followed a style of industrial management which had a great deal in common with the most unpleasant bureaucratic institutions. People were of little account, and increased profit was everything. In this factory Hugh had no future. All the modifications and improvements he had made were simply the property of the factory, and he had no claim on them. But Hugh knew the value of his inventions, and was filled with indignation.

Eventually he decided to make a stand, and when he was asked to work out new plans incorporating an improvement or adaptation, he simply copied old patterns and models without making any alterations, although he was fully aware of how improvements might be made. This did not go unnoticed, and Hugh soon received a note from the chief engineer, who casually observed that he had, it seemed, exhausted his talents.

"I am only a draftsman," said Hugh, "and I am paid even less than my predecessor, who did not invent a thing."

"Invent?" said the engineer. "What kind of inventor do you think you are? Your duty is to work out in detail the projects which are passed on to you. If all you can do is copy, we can soon find someone to take your place."

"Well, go and find him, then!" thought Hugh. And he

decided that from that day forward not a single invention of his would fall into the factory's hands.

His new attitude very soon had repercussions. At the end of that year he did not get a raise. During the next year his salary was cut. This meant that he could be dismissed as one who had "lost the capacity for work."

Hugh understood, but he was not prepared to give way.

Meanwhile, it should be noted that the relationship between Hugh and Madge was not prospering, and it became obvious that reality was not living up to their brilliant dreams, that life was dull. At first, Madge enjoyed thinking of Hugh as an "inventor," for it gratified her self-esteem; but later on she began to wish he was more like other men, and cared more for her and thought less about his fantasies. Not long after they were married, Madge began to think that Hugh took very little notice of her, left her too much on her own, rarely talked to her, and did not try to amuse or please her. Other husbands were more solicitous—and practical.

Actually Hugh was, of course, well aware of how things stood, but he did not want to admit failure and stubbornly pursued his ambition. Here the difference in their origins showed itself. Madge was like a house dog endowed with a good sense of smell, but lacking the endurance and persistence of a true hunting dog. Hugh, on the other hand, was of another breed. He hardly seemed to notice he was making any sacrifices and certainly did not regard them as such. Everything he did was done for *that,* and so why worry about it?

The tyranny of Hugh's obsession was hard for Madge to bear. Sacrificing everything himself, Hugh automatically demanded the same sacrifices from her. He got too used to a

certain way of thinking, and it was difficult for him to recognize Madge's point of view. He found it strange, for example, that Madge wanted to go to the theater. "How can
we justify going to the theater, *now?*" Hugh would ask
himself. "Later on we shall be able to see everything." But
Madge felt differently.

In the last two years her relationship with Hugh had
really begun to deteriorate—especially since she had lost
her job. She had not been able to find another, and now
had less money and more free time. She stayed at home
and was bored. Above all, she was suffering from not having children. Before the wedding Madge had believed that
somehow it would not be long before children came along.
Subsequently everything had appeared to her in another
light, and a very disagreeable one at that.

There are special demons concerned with the organization of people's family lives, manipulating, so to speak, the
intensity of effect of chance events in the family. These
demons could tell you better than I how and why it happened thus. I can say only one thing: people differ. Some
are either primitive to such a degree and others so perverted,
that they remain unaffected by pretense in matters of love.
Hugh and Madge were not sufficiently primitive to be satisfied with what fortune had bestowed on them, and at the
same time too sane to bend nature to their whim. Nature
began to take vengeance in the face of their futile attempts
at a relationship. What began as an imperceptible coolness
rapidly deteriorated as time progressed, and by the end of
the last year they were virtually strangers. It often occurred
to Madge that someone else in her place would long ago
have divorced Hugh and married an ordinary man. Hardest
to bear was the quarreling, already a long-standing habit.
At first to provoke Hugh, but later because she began to
believe it herself, Madge would insist that he did not love

her and that she was of no use to him. All attempts by
Hugh to impart his dreams and enthusiasm and tell her
about his prospects for the future invariably ended with
Madge crying, and shouting that she did not want to hear
a single word more.

Meanwhile, Hugh's inventions were not making much head-
way. Either they were not practical or Hugh was late apply-
ing for patents and found other inventors six months ahead
of him.

The latest of his inventions was a cunning device for
measuring and recording the speed of locomotives. It was
a necessary and practical invention: good instruments of
this kind were not to be had, and the Railway Company
was holding an open competition for the best design. Hugh
devised and made a remarkably practical machine combin-
ing high precision with a simple design. But he suffered a
setback here too. The principle, which he claimed was
unique, happened to have been used by another inventor,
who was ahead of him by only three weeks and won the
prize.

When Hugh heard this, for the first time in his life he
felt something like despair.

"Had I been free of my job, my model would have been
ready three months ago," he said to himself. "With this
millstone around my neck, I'll always just miss the boat,
and others will always get what was intended for me."

He wanted to tell Madge about this setback, but was
sure she would have no sympathy for him. She was too
violently opposed to his inventions. She would say that she
always knew that nothing would come of it, that he had
thrown away nearly a whole year, that she was right when
she said that money wasted on the workshop and the

models would have been far better spent on something else —a summer holiday or something to buy. They needed so many things!

What could he say to all this? Say again what he always said, that they must wait, that soon they would have everything they wanted. Hugh felt himself that words of this kind, far from calming and consoling Madge, would only irritate and offend her the more.

Going over everything, Hugh convinced himself that Madge had already reconciled herself to her present life and wished only to make a slight improvement upon it. At heart, of course, Hugh knew what Madge really wanted, but he knew too that it meant for him abandoning all attempts at invention and devoting all his time and effort to a job. To this he could not agree. His whole being rebelled and protested against it.

So it was, on the evening of the day he learned that the invention in which he had placed his faith had fallen through, that Hugh sat in his room and thought over what to do next. On the opposite wall hung an engraving he had bought some two years previously; it showed Prometheus chained to the rock with an eagle tearing out his liver. Prometheus—that was himself. The eagle was his place of work, daily draining his strength from him.

"Insofar as free labor is excellent, so is forced labor horrible," Hugh thought. "That savage creature is the forefather of our culture, who, instead of consuming his victim whole, makes him his slave. We are the victims slowly devoured by our conquerors."

You may observe that Hugh sometimes spoke in aphorisms.

At that moment, Madge returned home. She had been visiting the wife of one of the factory employees and in conversation had learned that Hugh's salary had been reduced. This had been two months before, and he had not mentioned it to her. Madge was sick at heart. First, there was his insincerity and then there was the worry of where it was all going to end. Hugh would be sacked! Madge was hurt and indignant on Hugh's behalf, but more than that, as usual, upset and filled with envy by the sight of her friend's three lively children.

Madge went home in a whirl of thoughts and decisions. She resolved to have a serious talk with Hugh. It was her duty. She had to save Hugh from himself. "He is like a drunkard or a gambler," she thought. "I shall tell him that I'll leave him if he won't give it up once and for all. If he loves me, he'll give it up."

Well, you can imagine what kind of talk they had.

"I must talk to you, Hugh," said Madge, entering his room and sitting down.

Hugh frowned.

"I've got to go out," he said.

"Wait a little. I never see you for weeks on end. I can't bear it any longer. I've been at Evelyn Johnson's. For God's sake! Do you know what they are saying about you at work? The Director says that you're either a drunkard or a drug addict. Why did you marry me if you have no need for me?"

It had come out quite differently from the way Madge had intended. Hugh's unwillingness to talk to her, when it was all his fault, made her explode uncontrollably.

Hugh was silent for several minutes while he listened to Madge; his face darkened. Then he began to speak, inter-rupting Madge. Madge went on talking and neither of them listened to the other, each trying to say his piece. Hugh said that Madge did not understand him and did not want to understand him; the factory interfered with his work; he must leave the office; if he had stuck it up to now, it was only for her sake; and now she was using some silly woman's gossip to persuade him that he was ruining his future. As if he had a future in that factory! A perfect niche for him, indeed.

"Evelyn is not at all a silly woman," Madge replied hotly. "She is a very clever woman and cleverer than you, however marvelous you think you are. To you everybody is a fool and an idiot. Only you have any brains. I just can't stand it any longer, I can't, can't, can't!"

Madge started sobbing.

And so, to be brief, things proceeded according to their usual pattern.

Hugh ended up smashing two chairs into splinters and leaving the house, banging the door so hard that it split down the middle. He then spent the rest of the evening drinking in a bar. He struck up an acquaintance with a company of out-of-work actors and stood them drinks all over town throughout the night. But the more Hugh drank, the more sober he became and the more clearly he understood his situation.

It was a dismal rainy morning when Hugh returned from his drinking bout, having decided not to go to work. The world seemed to be scraped bare, and Hugh saw very clearly all the exposed nerves and sinews of life. It was impossible to deceive himself that morning. The raw, unvarnished and undisguised truth of life was shrieking at him from all sides. "Yield, or you will be crushed!" screamed life. "It may already be too late; you may already have missed the moment to submit and perhaps even now you are already dead."

Hideous brick houses, wet asphalt streets; dull, everyday crowds, grimy and grotesque; cabbage peelings in rubbish bins; a drunken old man on crutches; ragged, shrill-voiced, filthy boys—all this Hugh saw as if for the first time. He had never imagined that life could be so ugly.

I am sure you are aware that the morning after a drinking bout can often have a very salutary effect, especially for a person with a strong stomach and clear head. The sick man cannot see the moral of the fable, but Hugh was healthy and he saw life bared to the quick.

Worst of all, his dreams seemed somehow to be glassy, lifeless, and artificial.

Without realizing it, Hugh returned home with a ready-made decision.

Madge was not at home. On the table lay a letter from her of some ten pages. It looked as though she had written the whole night through. "I am no use to you" was the main theme of her letter. "You have forgotten that I am a woman. I want to live, and I'm not interested in the future but the present." Madge concluded by saying that she had written to her aunt in California and hoped to go and stay with her.

Hugh started to answer the letter, but stopped on the second page. Then he tore up all that he had written and went to bed.

Drab days followed one upon the other. Several times Hugh tried to talk to Madge, but each time he met with failure. That key which makes it possible for people to talk to each other and come to a peaceful understanding seemed to have been lost. On two occasions they quarreled violently. After that, Hugh hardly went home at all. He could do no work either, and spent all his evenings in a bar.

Two or three weeks passed, and then one fine morning Hugh woke early with one idea in mind. There was nothing more to think about: it was time to act.

I had long been aware of the way his mind was tending; indeed, I noticed it before he did. People are often unaware of the presence of this thought; only very rarely do they grasp it in its entirety. You know of course what I am talking about: many vain people cherish the idea of putting an end to everything themselves in the event of things not turning out as they had planned. Each has his pet version of this thought; one sees before him a revolver, another a glass of poison. There is reassurance in these dreams, for life becomes bearable as soon as a man thinks of leaving it. Such thoughts give me great pleasure, because they assert my power over man. You may not be able to understand this, but a person who finds consolation in the thought of a revolver or a glass of poison believes in my power and considers that to be stronger than the self.

There is an unpleasant type of person to whom thoughts of this nature are completely foreign. These people do not believe in the reality of life; they take it for sleep. For them reality lies somewhere beyond the bounds of life. To kill oneself because of a setback in life is as absurd to this type of person as killing oneself after a chance visit to a moving play at the theater. I do not care for such people; fortunately, Hugh did not belong to this type. He had no doubts about the reality of life. The reality simply held no attraction for him. Hugh was an observant person, and he realized that he had been thinking about suicide for some time. Nevertheless, he too considered the deciding factors to be the failure of his last invention, the quarrel with Madge, and his steadily growing aversion to work. The cause, of course, lay elsewhere. Without his knowledge or conscious effort, the "thought" had fully developed in his mind and closed it to any alternatives. I like these moments in the life of a person. They constitute the ultimate triumph of matter, in the face of which man is powerless; and this powerlessness is never so complete and evident as in such moments.

This, then, is how matters stood. Hugh was a decisive, clear-headed person. All that had to be done he had already considered, weighed up, and calculated, and he did not want to put it off any longer. You know how one feels just before a journey, when one imagines one has already left, unable to bear even the thought of delay. Hugh woke up in just such a state on the morning with which I started my story.

Everything was well considered. Five years before, Hugh had insured his life, and Madge was due to receive the benefit even if he committed suicide. Hugh wrote her a short letter, left it in the unlocked drawer of his table, dressed, and left the house at the time he usually left for the office. But this time he traveled to town.

It was early. Hugh went to a café and had a hearty breakfast. I had no fears about him. He was cool, resolute, and calm. Leaving the café, he took the elevated railway downtown to Broadway. With hands thrust into the pockets of his overcoat, he sat and viewed the faces of the other passengers with a faint expression of disgust. It was an ordinary morning crowd—people hurrying to work, to the office, to banks and stores. Hugh looked at them and in his mind formed something resembling the prayer of the Pharisee: "Thank you, Lord, for making me not like them; thank you for giving me strength to resist my slavery; give me strength to depart." The vacant faces were telling Hugh what he would have been reduced to had he not possessed an ever-active spirit of protest, a will to fight, and a reluctance to accept failure. Every now and then Hugh's face froze with contempt and he reminded me of the American Indian of times past who, defying surrender, sings a final song before throwing himself from the cliff into the abyss.

"Slaves," thought Hugh, "slaves, who are not even conscious of their slavery. They have already got used to it. They never dreamed of better things; never even felt the desire for freedom. They have never even thought about freedom. Great God, just to think that I might have become like that! So long as I believed that I could overcome, I was content to bear it, but now it's all over. There is no escape from slavery, and I refuse to be a slave. As it is, I have suffered too long."

Disdainfully he observed the comings and goings of the passengers. He was conscious of his superiority and he felt strong. People would go on with their dull and tedious lives, the trains would continue to run, the slaves would hurry to work; the rain would fall and it would be miserable, wet, and cold. While for him, by tomorrow, all this would be no more. A shot on the seashore muffled by the wind and rain, a knock on the chest—and that is all. Such should be the end for all defeated braves.

I noticed that Hugh felt easy in his mind, much more relaxed than the day before, and I rejoiced, because all this brought him nearer to the moment of my triumph, that is, the triumph of Great Matter, or the Great Deception, over the spirit, will, and consciousness of man. Psychologically this moment is exceedingly interesting. In order to come to it, the person must believe unconditionally in the reality of that which actually does not exist, in the reality of myself and my reign. You understand? Suicide is the result of infinite faith in matter. If a person has even the slightest doubts, harbors only the faintest suspicion that a deception is being practiced, he will not kill himself. To carry out his intention he must believe that everything that seems to exist, is.

Imagine my delight, therefore, when he has already performed his last gesture—pulled the trigger, jumped

over the parapet, or swallowed the poison; when realizing
that everything is finished and there is no turning back,
suddenly lightning strikes: he has made a mistake; everything is not as it seemed, all is upside down, there is no
reality but the one blessing that he has thrown away—that
is, life itself. He is overwhelmed by the realization that he
has committed an act of folly that cannot be reversed, and
convulsively gropes about for something to hang onto, to
drag himself out of the pit, to return at the last moment. To
me, this is beautiful! Nothing gives me such pleasure. If
only you could appreciate what is going on in the soul of a
man at that moment; how he longs then to take one, only
one, single step backwards . . .

However, to return to Hugh.

He got out of the train at Broadway, descended to the
street, and went to one of the largest gun shops. I could
read his thoughts. Hugh wanted to buy the very best revolver.

My friend, you blame us for much of what happens to you.
But if you only knew how little does depend on us. Take
this case. Had I known the outcome of his purchase of the
revolver, I should have advised Hugh from the bottom of
my heart to stop at a chemist to buy some poison for a sick
dog. Yes, had I known what was going to happen, perhaps
I would have guided him to the drugstore in person. I will
be honest with you and confess that, generally speaking,
no devil can make head or tail of you humans. Sometimes
you fill me with indignation to the depth of my soul, sometimes you bring me intense joy just at the moment I am
least expecting it.

What occurred in the shop was one of the most unpleasant incidents in my life: never before had I felt quite
so stupid and helpless.

Here is how it happened.

Hugh entered the shop and asked to see a revolver which was handy for the pocket and had a good action, not too big, not too small, and of the latest make. The salesman brought out about ten different revolvers, and Hugh started to scrutinize them, as if it was important to him to choose the right one to shoot himself with.

At first I did not pay attention to it and put it down to normal eccentricity. You understand I have to be present at such selections every now and then in the line of professional duty, so I stood aside and whiled away the time with other thoughts. At length, I noticed that Hugh was taking too long to choose the revolver, and I became bored with waiting. I approached him, and saw something entirely unexpected.

Hugh had changed; here was a completely different person from the one that had entered the shop a few minutes before. You will not understand this, but we know that each of you has several faces; we even call the faces by different names. Imagine, therefore, entering a shop with one person and five minutes later encountering quite a different one. Our life is full of such changes. I was infuriated, particularly because I could see that the thought which had led him here (upon the development of which, I must confess, I had worked not a little) suddenly paling and shrinking so that I could hardly find it in the jostling crowd of new thoughts thrusting themselves into his consciousness. I could see, too, that all these new thoughts were edging my "thought" into a corner; and I realized that all of them had occurred during the time that Hugh was in the shop. Worst of all, these thoughts were all of a completely incomprehensible technical nature and I was at a loss what to do with them.

There was a pile of revolvers and repeating rifles on the counter, and with burning eyes and a happy, animated expression, Hugh was speaking loudly about something to the two salesmen. They seemed to have become interested in the inquisitive buyer and had taken out all sorts of rifles and revolvers of new makes and novel systems to show him. I had little idea what they were talking about, because it consisted of technical terms such as "recoil" and "breakthrough of gases." Apparently all this interested them very much.

Finally Hugh fell silent, and with intense concentration, began to open and close a short cartridge chamber, only now and then exchanging remarks with the salesman. I saw him wholly preoccupied with some new thought which had swept everything else away. A new invention! Can you credit it? Something had appeared in his brain during these few minutes, and that something had conquered all his fine intentions. When I tried to work out what was in his mind, I was at a loss. "Escape of gases" and "utilization of recoil" were the two main thoughts, like wheels turning in his brain moving him on to various other technical considerations, formulas, and calculations. All this was completely outside my field, you understand. I knew only that it concerned some new type of revolver or gun. Of course, I cannot be totally indifferent to developments in this area—such a subject is of consuming interest to me. However, I did not trust Hugh's enthusiasm; he would always get carried away and then it would turn out that the enterprise was not worth a damn. And I was very upset by Hugh's change of mood. As I have already told you, I approved of his decision. He was close to a very beautiful jump downwards, into the unknown; and I had planned how, while he was somersaulting in space, I would make his soul turn inside out with anguish and despair. It is always so comic! On the other hand, I could not pass over his new thought without proper consideration. This was more than a gadget for measuring the speed of engines! It was, indeed, well worth taking up. But here I came up against a barrier. You see, you people are all too clever for me. However hard I tried to penetrate Hugh's thoughts, I could make nothing of them, except something about a rod with a spiral spring, which for some reason was of paramount importance.

Try to understand my position.

Had Hugh thought of something interesting *per se,* forging a will, say, or seducing an innocent girl, or planting a bomb in a theater, I could have helped him, and very substantially at that. But here in this rod with the spiral spring there was absolutely nothing of, how shall I put it . . . an emotional nature. Here was a detail of a new invention and nothing else. There was no crime in that; and I can only get busy when an enterprise has a whiff of crime about it. It became apparent to me that I was doomed to total passivity, although at the same time I could see that Hugh's new idea might prove to be very useful from the point of view of crime in general. This instance illustrates the sort of predicament in which I've often found myself of late. A great deal is happening behind my back and without my help. You have become too cunning for me. In the good old days I knew everything and was able to anticipate. Nowadays I find myself bewildered by technical progress.

To return to my story: In the end Hugh bought a revolver and cartidges, put them in his pocket, and went out of the shop.

I noticed that he went out very differently from the way he had come in. You will not understand this—even if you grasp it intellectually, you still cannot *see*—but we see that a man walks in many different ways. The man who decides to shoot himself walks entirely differently from the one to whom a thought about a new invention has occurred. It would take too long to explain, but we find it oddly comical that the same word *walk* can apply in both these instances.

To continue: It was very sad for me to see Hugh in this new persona. Would something interesting result from his new invention or not? I could not then know the answer; but I was well aware that here was a most curious case apparently escaping my control. And you know I always reckon that a bird in the hand is better than two in the bush. It is my favorite saying.

Hugh went out into the street. His whole mind was filled with his newly hatched thoughts, buzzing about like bees. However, acting upon a strong impulse peculiar to strong-willed people, Hugh still made his way toward the originally decided place.

Suddenly I found myself thinking, "Who knows? I must see this to the end." Sometimes it happens that a person who has cherished the thought of suicide shoots or hangs himself long after all the original reasons for the thought have disappeared. This is merely the work of the thought itself, which has become independent and has subordinated its author.

I remember one woman who had decided to poison herself if her lover did not return from the war. She had a small bottle of poison which she kissed every night before going to sleep. Her lover returned whole and unharmed, and on the very first night of his return, she drank the poison and died before his eyes.

Hugh again caught the elevated train, then the electric tram, changed several times, took a long walk, and finally ended up on a deserted beach, having left the town, harbor, and warehouses far behind him. The place he had arrived at was a dreary and desolate stretch of sand and sea. One could not have thought anywhere more suitable for suicide. On the right stood the charred remains of a warehouse which had burned down the year before. Nothing else was to be seen.

By now it had stopped raining. Hugh sat down on a stone not far from the water, took out a notebook, and started to scribble down notes and drawings. I looked over his shoulder several times but I could see nothing but numbers and symbols. These I could not understand, and it became tedious.

Finally Hugh put the notebook into his pocket and got up, looking proud and resolute, as if he had come to a decision. "No, devil take it, I am not beaten yet," he said. "I know that I shall win in the end, and I have always known it. Cowardice and faintheartedness have led me here! This new idea will give me my freedom, cost what it may."

He took the revolver, loaded it, climbed onto a boulder facing the sea, lifted his arm, and, as if challenging someone to a fight, released six shots one after the other into the misty horizon. Then he clicked the lock, threw out the blackened, smoldering cartridge cases, looked at them with a smile, put the revolver into his pocket, and went back to town.

Imagine such a scene, and consider what a fool I had been made to feel.

Hugh did not get home until the evening. A surprise awaited him: Madge had left. On the table was a letter from her, and keys.

"Dear Hugh," she wrote, "do not be angry with me for going away without saying goodbye. It would have been very difficult, because I do love you very much, whatever happens. But I feel I am no use to you and am even in your way. For some time now you have taken no notice of me, and when you do, you make me feel like a tiresome fly which is buzzing around and preventing you from working. Perhaps it is all my fault that I do not understand your thoughts, but I cannot agree to sacrifice the present for the sake of what perhaps will never be. I feel sorry for everything that we have lost, and am constantly in tears over the babies we could have had and whom we did not allow to be born in this world. I know what you will say, but I simply cannot believe you any longer. I realize that you have ceased to love me. I will live with my aunt in Los Angeles and will always think of you. Goodbye, Hugh."

As you can see, a most touching and sentimental letter.

Her letter acted strongly on Hugh.

"And I wanted to shoot myself," said he. "I should be hanged merely for having had such a thought. Poor Madge. How fortunate that she did not find my silly letter. Well, let her stay in California for a while. It is possibly better that way. I will work. And devil take me if I do not get my way."

He did not go to bed until very late. First he wrote a letter to Madge, a very affectionate and tender one. He asked her to wait a year for him, and promised to come when the year was up, either triumphant or resolved to leave inventions forever and start a new life with Madge in the West. "Everything will be all right, my dear Madge," he wrote, "only do not think that I do not love you or need you."

Then he spent some time working out his finances—a simple job. He had two thousand dollars in savings. One thousand he decided to send to Madge, the other thousand he would live on himself. He would leave his job.

Then he plunged into calculations in connection with his new idea and spent the rest of the night sketching, drafting, and calculating; finally, exhausted, he threw down the pencil and sat for a long time with his eyes closed, seeing something I could not see.

"Yes," he said finally, "seven bullets in two seconds, two seconds for loading, one hundred and five bullets in a min-

ute if the bullets are made in nickel casing; with the saving
of all gases it will have a force totally inconceivable in a
single revolver."

These were the first intelligent words I had heard from
him during the whole day.

"One hundred and five bullets in a minute," I reflected,
"and in a nickel casing at that. Not bad."

Hugh went to bed. He was a person without imagination, and thought little about the wonderful benefits his
invention could have for the whole of humanity. Involuntarily I was carried away. One hundred and five bullets a
minute! This idea was indeed worthy of praise. I could appreciate it at its true value.

Next morning Hugh sent off the letter and money to Madge
and sat down to work. One day followed another without
incident. From morning onwards Hugh sat at the drawing
board or at his bench, cutting out various parts, testing, and
altering; the evenings he spent in a bar, sitting drinking
beer and smoking his pipe. He had left his job, and nothing
interested him except his work and his letters from Madge.
At first Madge wrote seldom, but later on she began to miss
Hugh and he came to appear much more attractive to her.
She started to write nearly every day, describing California,
the sea, the heat, the sun, and asking Hugh to come sooner,
so that they could work together and build the future for
themselves and the children which they would certainly
have sometime.

"Leave New York sooner, dear Hugh," she wrote, "and
come here. We have been parted by the gray mists, dust, and
smoke of the city, but the sun will bring us closer to each
other again."

Madge rather liked reading poetry and expressing herself elegantly. She thought herself to be much more educated than Hugh. The truth was she swallowed a great number of books whole.

Hugh read the letters, wrote brief answers, and continued to work. But in his heart of hearts he would have liked to leave everything to go to Madge in California, to try a completely new life amidst nature, a struggle against the elements.

He imagined a mountain covered with pine forests. On a ledge of the mountain stood a simple log cabin and there was Madge waving to him from the porch. He remembered novels by Bret Harte, although he knew that contemporary California had become a completely different country. But most of all he dreamed of Madge. He was a strange chap, married five years and still in love with his wife. When they were together, quarrels, disagreements, and mutual misunderstandings smothered his love. But from a distance Madge again seemed to him to shine with all the colors of the rainbow, and Hugh went back to believing that there was no woman more beautiful, charming, tempting, and clever than Madge. It was true that there was much they disagreed about, but this was only because Madge's soul was striving for truth, freedom, and beauty. His was striving toward the same goal, but by a longer and more difficult road. She, with the inner wisdom of womanhood, would find what she was looking for in the sun, in nature, in her longing for children. And this was right and good. But Hugh was not an American for nothing, and continued to think that a million dollars added to all this would make it even better. And if his dreams came true, then Madge would agree with him and admit that it had been worth the effort and sacrifice of all these years.

· · ·

A month passed, then another, a third, then half a year, and at last the day came when Hugh had a rough draft ready.

The result of all this labor, thinking, calculating, enthusiasm, persistence, effort of will, sleepless nights, and visions was the birth of a rather awkward little creature. It was the automatic pistol. From the outside it resembled a hammer or a spanner more than a revolver. But it undoubtedly had many new features which promised a great future. I recognized that at once. What interested me, though, was whether anything of it would come Hugh's way. So often it is not the inventors who profit from their inventions.

The pistol was flat and heavy. Seven bullets were located not in the drum, but in the handle. The shock from the shot slid back the top part of the pistol; at the same time the case of the spent cartridge was ejected to the side and a new cartridge was inserted into the barrel, fed by a spring from below. All very clever and practical. The firing speed far exceeded anything known at the time, and because there was no escape of gases between the drum and the barrel, it was nearly three times as powerful as a revolver of the same caliber.

The conception had not been without its setbacks. Hugh had struggled long with the extractor for the spent cartridges. Then he was very concerned about the safety lock, and this remained the weak spot of the child born in Hugh's workshop. Altogether a time of anxieties and doubts.

When I understood exactly what kind of a child was to be born, my attitude toward Hugh's work improved considerably. But as I have already told you, there was no way in which I could help because there was absolutely nothing of interest for me in his thoughts or his feelings; that is, there was nothing in the slightest degree criminal. You understand, the field of my activities is limited by the emotions involved. I cannot go out of this field any more than a fish can fly or a bird swim under water. Some of my colleagues have tried to pose as flying fish or diving birds, but nothing has ever come of it. We are creatures of a definite elemental force. Hugh was completely immune to this force. I have already told you that he had not the faintest hint of imagination in the sense that I understand it. In fact, to be honest, I was often extremely embarrassed by his dreams of Madge, of love, of freedom, of all their future happiness and prosperity. It was all so insipid and sickening.

Madge began to write more often. She was happy in California; she had decided to learn the flower trade and was working on a flower farm belonging to her aunt's husband.

"I will give you a year's grace, Hugh," she wrote. "After a year, with inventions or without, you must be here; we will rent land and grow flowers."

Hugh sighed over these letters, put them away in his writing table, and went to his bench. You cannot imagine how funny you people are sometimes.

So, finally, Hugh's child was born—ungainly, but with enormous hidden potential, and a great future. Of this I was certain.

It was, I believe, exactly six months after that misty morning on which Hugh had taken the bus to the seashore. Now he was on his way there again and by the same road, but in a completely different mood. Again and again he would touch the heavy object in his pocket and experience the thrill of triumph. He also had with him two thick square oak boards, a target, and a range-finder constructed in his spare time. This load pleased him. He had no doubts about results. The crowd of morning travelers hurrying to work now moved him to pity, mixed with contempt; no longer did he fear being one of them.

"I wonder," thought Hugh, "how it is that we have not started castrating your kind. If only some billionaire were to come to the conclusion that castrated employees are more useful than whole ones, I am sure that many would willingly undergo a small operation; parents would send their children to the hospital to secure them employment in the future. Perhaps one soul out of ten thousand would realize what is happening; the rest will think they are alive and will in all seriousness regard themselves as people. I too would have been such a one had I not been prepared to die ten times over rather than live a life without freedom and my own independent work."

Hugh certainly did not show any special modesty at that moment, and this gave me great pleasure. You see, I was not worried for the child, it was Hugh I was not so sure of. It seemed to me that he had many flaws and would face severe trials. The future proved this to be true.

The fate of inventors, painters, poets, and people of this breed in general is very interesting. To be honest, nothing gave me greater pleasure for many a long year than the case of a French painter who shot himself in poverty and failure; only a few years later his pictures were sold for hundreds of thousands. This was delightful. People had not yet lost their sense of humor. And I did all I could to awaken the consciousness of this painter "on the other side" and give him the good news. It was splendid to see how he received it. When he understood me, he nearly choked himself with fury—and would have done so, had he been able to breathe. But there was nothing he could do because, strictly speaking, he did not exist. Nevertheless, he felt the comedy of it. Truly, I would not wish his astral mantle upon you. He has poisoned himself for millions of years with his anger toward people. Think of it, five years after the death of the man who shot himself because of hunger, to pay a million francs for his pictures! Wasn't that marvelous?

But I am digressing. I had hopes of something of this sort for Hugh, and soon my prophecies began to come true.

But that particular morning everything went as Hugh expected. I can't tell you now exactly how many shots a minute there were at the first trial and how many inches deep they penetrated into the board. But Hugh was jubilant. The force of action of the pistol was equal to that of a large rifle, and the speed of shots exceeded that of a machine gun, which at that time took a long time to load.

All Hugh's calculations proved to be splendidly correct. The conduct of the child was irreproachable. It could now be exposed to judgment by people, and people judged by it. Hugh returned home glowing with inner exultation. To-morrow would begin the triumphal procession.

But reality bade differently. The first thing Hugh realized was that he had no money. Indeed, not only had he no money, but he had already accumulated a number of small debts. The matter of money came up when Hugh started thinking about patents. From experience he knew a patent is costly: one needs models . . . drawings . . . the Patent Office demands a considerable sum in advance. Foreign patents were particularly expensive.

"Damnation," said Hugh, "it's a complete mess."

There was only one thing he could sell: the insurance policy.

"It would be absurd to keep it now," said Hugh. "Even if I die, Madge is sure to receive more from the child than the price of my life."

By evening the policy was sold. Hugh ordered the various parts of the models to be made in different workshops, and the various parts of the plans to be drawn in different drafting offices. Oh, he was cautious! He assembled the models himself and wrote all the inscriptions to the drawings in his own hand. This work took about a month and used up nearly all the money gained from the sale of the policy. "Now," Hugh said to himself at last, "it is time to secure the destiny of the child."

It was just at this point that the greatest obstacle appeared, one which Hugh had failed to foresee and was completely unprepared for, but which I knew well, simply from previous experience. This was the struggle against the essential apathy of life. The world is reluctant to admit the new. When the new arrives, it is seldom, very seldom, that it finds an unobstructed path. Disappointments and difficulties are the customary reward of those who bring in the new. But Hugh was not prepared for this and naively expected that the millions were already piling up for him.

Hugh began by writing letters to all the big arms factories. He received no reply. He wrote again, inquiring about the arrival of his letters. Nobody answered. Hugh went in person to one factory. The Director was busy. The secretary who came out to speak to him said that offers of new inventions were discussed in the factory by a special committee three times a year, that the next meeting was due in two months' time, and that presentation of drawings and models was required. All this the secretary reeled off like a lesson learned by heart. It was obvious that she often had to deal with inventors.

"Haven't you got someone here who understands the technicalities who could simply try out my pistol?" asked Hugh.

The secretary smiled faintly at this impudence and said that all inventors demanded immediate trials and that in order not to waste time, the factory had a set routine, and testing was carried out only on inventions which had been approved by the committee. With that she bade Hugh a good day, sir!

"Of course, I could not have expected it to be otherwise," Hugh said to himself. "Why should these corpses suddenly come to life? What a fool I am not to have thought of this before. It's not letter-writing that is needed, but going out and looking in person. There must be live people somewhere. A live man will understand instantly."

Hugh started to call on factories.

The results were about the same as those of his first interview. Models and drawings were requested, and he was asked to call again in a month's time. But Hugh did not want to give away his model. He was not at all sure that his patent protected all the details of the invention. He knew how easy it was to make a few alterations and take out a new patent, and the impossibility of a penniless and unknown inventor bringing a lawsuit against a large corporation. Imitations would not be dangerous once he had conquered the market; meanwhile, nobody would be given the model. Yet without seeing the model, nobody was prepared even to talk.

Madge wrote seldom. It seemed to Hugh that, absorbed in her new interests in life, she had begun to forget him.

Another two months passed. Hugh was at the end of his money. He left his apartment and went to live in a small room.

It was on a very hot day during one of those New York heat waves, after Hugh had called without success at two factories and at a bureau for new inventors, that he wandered aimlessly down several streets and into Central Park.

A badly dressed gray-haired man with a mocking, clever face sat down on the same bench as Hugh, and they began talking. For some reason Hugh felt drawn to this stranger. During the day the parks of New York reveal a whole gallery of human ruins, and this man was obviously one of them. Hugh offered him a cigar. He felt depressed and wanted to hear a human voice. The gray-haired man said something amusing about the passers-by; he was, apparently, perceptive and witty. Hugh took him to be a failed writer or artist and invited him for a glass of beer.

In the bar it was cool and neither of them had any desire to leave. After several cold beers, the older man began to speak about himself. Hugh's heart was chilled when he heard that he was an inventor. The more he listened, the more it seemed that he heard his own story, with a terrible, hopeless end. The old man went on talking and Hugh listened to him, inwardly freezing with terror, and at the same time, out of some morbid curiosity, inquiring into details. It was all so familiar: youth, proud dreams, love, work, success, and then suddenly the senseless and incomprehensible end of everything. A splendid invention—which made someone else's fortune—the total inability to gain recognition for one's rights, poverty, drink, casual work, and then the knowledge that it was already past history, some ten, no, some fifteen years ago.

Hugh knew that such tales could be heard from a great many people whose acquaintance one makes in the park. All these people, with the experience of misfortune behind them, have similar stories, both real and fictitious. It could very well be that this man was making it all up, that he was obsessed with an invention which had never been. But this did not distract Hugh. What mattered to him was that the man called himself an inventor. And even if it was all a story, it was morbidly realistic.

"If my affairs go well, I must help him," Hugh said to himself. And the *if* frightened him.

"Damn it, in ten years' time I too may be telling someone in a bar about my invention." Hugh shivered.

Hugh wrote down the old man's address—the name of

a tobacconist in one of the slum quarters. On the way home Hugh suddenly felt afraid of life again.

Oh, I knew that he would come to this.

Life did not want to acknowledge him and his invention, and Hugh began to realize more fully and clearly the fact that everything he had accomplished so far—the inventing, the work, the patents—was trifling compared with the difficulty of introducing an invention into life.

He remembered a book he had once read about inventions and discoveries which had been made a long time ago and then forgotten; he even stopped on the pavement, talking to himself: "Steam engines were discovered in Roman times, a medieval monk discovered electricity; how many more will there be?"

That day Hugh returned home with his tail between his legs. A letter from Madge awaited him. Madge had only one thing to ask him: he was to write her the truth—that he no longer loved her—and then she would not think of him any more and would cease to annoy him with her silly letters.

This letter pierced Hugh to the heart. To write and tell Madge she was wrong was futile. Hugh knew this very well; besides, he had simply run out of words. Words seemed worn out and useless. Hugh must go to Madge; otherwise, Madge would go from him and fall in love with someone else. This worried him for quite some time.

"What shall I do, if everything happens as I anticipate and there is no Madge?" he asked himself. The thought always made him feel physically cold. "It does happen in life," he told himself, "that everything a man wants comes, just a day too late."

Yes, life began to frighten Hugh in earnest.

He was now selling his very last possessions, things like watches and instruments. He continued on his rounds, terrified now to see many other inventors besides himself calling at the offices and factories. To the employees of these factories all of them stood on the lowest rung. They were not asked to sit down, they were sometimes not even let in, no one bothered to talk to them. On the door of one there was a notice which read: *To Advertisement Carriers, To All Those Asking For Work And To Inventors, Entrance Forbidden.*

Hugh had not come across this before.

In all this time, Hugh had had only two or three offers to buy the patent, but for such pitiful sums it would have been absurd to accept. He came to realize he was knocking his head against a wall, and that in the end he would come back to his first decision and, so that his invention should not perish in vain, would shoot himself with the new pistol. Indeed, everything pointed to such a course of action. A month or two more and Hugh would have done it. His patience had run out. But then a chance encounter seemed for a time to turn the tide.

In a small restaurant he frequented, Hugh met an old friend with whom he had attended evening classes to study mechanics. It turned out that this man—his name was Jones—had a small factory for making bicycle parts. He told Hugh how badly the business was going and how impossible it was to stand up to the syndicates who were swallowing up small enterprises; he had been fighting as long as he could and had now come to New York to sell his factory to a big group of companies. The group knew the precarious state of his affairs and he would have to agree to any conditions they stipulated; they had deliberately delayed the deal so that he would be forced virtually to give away the business to pay his debts.

Preoccupied, Hugh was only half listening to him, but then although he seldom discussed his affairs with others, he told Jones all about his invention and his setbacks.

Jones was interested, and Hugh invited him home— more because he did not want to be alone than for any other reason. The child made a big impression on his friend. At a glance he understood everything that was hidden behind its strange exterior. Then he set his mind to thinking of a way around the problem.

Early the following morning Jones came to Hugh.

"I have been thinking all night," he said. "Might it not be possible to adapt my factory to producing your device? This is possibly the last chance for both of us. I'm certain that the sharks, having no intention of letting me go free, have marked me down to be swallowed whole. If everything goes on as it is at present, in a year's time I shall probably be no more than a foreman in my own factory. They will not even take me as a manager."

Together they started to dismantle the child, thinking about which parts could be produced at Jones's factory and which would have to go elsewhere. Later, taking the range-finder and target, they went out to test the pistol, again taking the road to the shore.

Once out there Hugh demonstrated to Jones everything his child was capable of and with secret joy saw the eager expression on his companion's face. Jones himself started to shoot, sometimes with the range-finder and sometimes without, getting the child so hot that it could not be touched. Finally he slapped Hugh on the shoulder and said:

"Well, old man, I am yours. I will stake my last penny on this. I can hold out for six months. In that time we will win America, Europe, Asia, Africa, and Australia. There can never have been such an invention as this. I am yours to command!"

They started working together. Hugh took heart. The conversion of the factory worked well. After two months the first batch of automatic pistols was on the market. But the price had to be fixed rather high and the demand was low.

The factory was in full production, but after two months it became evident that the market was already saturated and repeat orders would take time. Jones borrowed money; advertisements and posters were very expensive, but it was clear that without an all-out publicity campaign the business would fail. All the large gun shops had the automatic pistols on show, but the public still preferred to buy revolvers.

Six months had passed since production had started, and Hugh and Jones were facing bankruptcy and an ignominious end to their collaboration. Two arms factories were prepared to buy the patent. One offered ten thousand dollars, the other less, but this did not even cover Jones's losses.

The strange pistol, resembling a hammer, even when exhibited in shop windows did not attract the public—only some unusual publicity stunt could save the day, and the company had not the means.

These were the blackest days of Hugh's life. He gave up, feeling only, with aching heart, that now he would not even have the strength to shoot himself.

But a great future awaited the child.

And finally it came! The seeds, scattered all over the world, at last fell on good earth!

All great reputations are made in Paris. And on this occasion too it turned out to be so.

The time I speak of saw a star of the first magnitude rising over the horizon of Europe.

Her name was Marion Gray.

A career equal to that of Patti was predicted for her. Her success in all the capital cities of Europe exceeded everything remembered for a decade. She had indeed an exceptional voice, but even without the voice, she would have been known throughout Europe for the scandals associated with her name. Wherever she went, her route was marked and followed by a trail of fantastic stories about her lovers and devotees, of duels, suicides, bankruptcies, and madmen.

To look at, Marion was a very thin and fragile blonde with a sad face and big childish eyes. She was the cause of a German prince of a reigning dynasty shooting himself, as a result of which Marion was expelled from Germany; she caused two Hungarian countesses in Budapest—mother and daughter—to commit suicide. At her door could be laid a number of gloomy duels and murders in Italy, reminiscent of the Renaissance. It was said that she took away with her the favorite odalisque of the Sultan, who later jumped into the sea from a yacht in the Mediterranean and drowned. She was at the root of some terrible drama in St. Petersburg, vague rumors of which were reported in foreign newspapers.

In short, Marion was the cause of everything worth talking about which had happened in Europe over the last two or three years. How much of these stories was truth and how much was invented, even I cannot tell you. All I can tell you is that Marion's fame grew by leaps and bounds.

That season she was singing in Paris. On her first night a young dragoon officer, a member of the Jockey Club and descendant of one of the most renowned French families, shot himself in the foyer of the Grand Opera House. Marion continued to sing and the connoisseurs said she sang as never before. The following day all the newspapers were full of the story of the tragic love of the young officer, and in a few days' time Marion's private life monopolized the press.

The whole of Paris knew well that Marion's chief love that season was an American, Miss Stockton, a writer whose novel depicting the Chinese underworld in San Francisco had created a big sensation not long before.

Miss Stockton drank whisky mixed half and half with ether, rode like a cowboy, and took part in public boxing matches as a champion middleweight. She was also the soul of jealousy. When she got drunk (nearly daily), she would beat Marion up and follow her about creating scenes and scandals.

Marion Gray's second string was Lord Tilbury, a fabulously rich Englishman, till then a quiet middle-aged man of even temper, a traveler and sportsman who shot tigers in India point-blank without batting an eyelid. It was said that he had spent in one season half his fortune on Marion and that it was likely he would spend the lot. Not since the time of the Second Empire had Paris seen such a shower of gold.

Miss Stockton aroused in Lord Tilbury a frenzied hatred; often he sat for nights on end with his tiger gun on his knees, his eyes staring distractedly, his thoughts on Miss Stockton. Miss Stockton knew of his hatred and retaliated in kind, vowing she would beat him up in public.

Besides these two, Marion had many other lovers and admirers. Her latest flame was a young Swedish diplomat, a spiritualist and clairvoyant, completely unbalanced. He communed with "spirits," caught falling stars in his hands, made Marion a present of an "astral lion" which only he could see, and so on.

Marion was fascinated. (Her enthusiasms were matched only by her unpredictability.) She arranged séances with

the Swede. The spirits ordered her to become his mistress—
she obeyed without delay. Then the spirits ordered her to
drive away Miss Stockton—and she did. Then the spirits
demanded the presence at the séances of Lord Tilbury
dressed as an Assyrian magician, and a certain French poet
was asked to be present. Further, the séances were to take
place in a gloomy dungeon with twenty-seven coffins containing real skeletons. (Lord Tilbury was entrusted with
the task of furnishing the coffins and skeletons.) But there
occurred an event which the spirits evidently had not fore-
seen.

It was past midnight when Miss Stockton burst into Marion's house. Two footmen, obeying instructions, barred her
way. Miss Stockton parried one of them with such a blow
that he flew head first into the fireplace; the other one got
a kick in the stomach and collapsed. Miss Stockton darted
up the stairs. She was drunk as a lord.

It happened that the door into the room where the
séance was being held was not locked. The Swedish diplomat, the French poet, Lord Tilbury, and Marion were seated
around a smoldering mixture of opium, aloe, and worm-
wood. The men were dressed, as the spirits commanded, in
red cloaks, while Marion was clad only in garlands of red
roses; the room was furnished in red. The coffins were still
missing.

Miss Stockton flung the door open, and seeing Marion
naked amidst the red roses, burst into a torrent of vile swear-
words, painstakingly learned from her cowboy friends. Lord
Tilbury jumped up to face her. I can assure you he looked
extremely handsome in his Assyrian hat and false beard.

From a leather holster under her jacket, Miss Stockton
drew the new automatic pistol and shot Lord Tilbury point-

blank in the chest; then she shot the Swedish diplomat through the head; loosed three bullets into Marion's back as she tried to flee; wounded the poet in the leg (he had the wit at this point to pretend to be dead); and with the seventh and last charge shot herself.

FOUR CORPSES! SEVEN SHOTS! shouted the Paris headlines the following day.

DEATH AMIDST ROSES. BLOODBATH ON THE CHAMPS-ÉLYSÉES!

BLACK MASS ON CHAMPS-ÉLYSÉES! TRAGIC DEATH OF A FAMOUS SINGER!

You can imagine what the Paris newspapers made of it. The public thrilled with horror at the special feature of the crime, the instrument of death—the new American pistol. Several newspapers printed photographs and descriptions of the pistol, while *Echo de Paris* and another newspaper even printed stories on the inventor, Hugh B. Moreover, each carried quite different photographs: a middle-aged Yankee with a stiff upper lip glared ferociously from one newspaper, while another—with the same caption—showed the portrait of a well-known American philanthropist.

For a whole week the newspapers were engrossed with Marion Gray, Miss Stockton, the Swedish diplomat, and Lord Tilbury. And not a single article, in any newspaper, missed the opportunity of mentioning the new American invention—the "diabolical device, new from our century of steam and electricity," as it was called by one newspaper. Which was bad grammar to start with, and secondly, quite ridiculous. All I could do was shrug my shoulders. What had I to do with it?

Then began the interviews with the young poet, who for the first week was thought to be on the verge of death or insanity, I don't remember which. A detachment of *ser-*

gents de ville was detailed to the hospital where he was lying. The poet gave some confused account of his role in the proceedings and of his relations with Marion. But later on—you can imagine why—he decided against reticence. The book he published two months after the event clearly implied that the drama's star was actually the author himself and his romance with Marion, with its undertones of mystery and Satanism. This book sold tens of thousands of copies and served as the first rung of the ladder which in time led the author into the Académie Française.

But all this came later. Meanwhile, before the day had ended, the telegraph wires were sending news of the bloody drama around the world. American newspapers reprinted whole pages wired from Europe, and although they did not like to give Hugh free advertising, it was after all an American invention and somehow it happened that Hugh's name was mentioned in every article. For several days Hugh became the pride of America.

The first and direct result of the incident was that gun shops everywhere were sold out of automatic pistols in a few days. Orders doubled and the Automatic Fire-Arm Company was snowed under with demands. Jones told Hugh that they must expand the business.

The next day a gentleman from one of the largest arms factories called at their office with an offer to buy the patent. Hugh remembered that it was the very company that had previously offered him a thousand dollars for the patent.

"What is your offer?" asked Hugh.

"Five hundred thousand," said the representative.

"We are not selling," said Hugh.

"We will buy the factory, machinery, patents, and all. I can bid up to a million."

Hugh said harshly, "We are not selling at any price."

And when the gentleman had departed, Jones slapped Hugh on the shoulder: "Well, old man, now our time has come. We have withstood the seven lean years, now will begin the seven fat ones. You can order your yacht." He knew about Hugh's daydreams, but Hugh was dreaming, not of yachts, but of Madge.

Orders poured in from all over the world. It was obvious that the factory could not produce in six months the amount required in one. Hugh and Jones found a financial genius who arranged a two-million-dollar issue of shares for them. On the strength of this, the banks advanced the capital they needed, and a delay in production was avoided.

Barely a month had passed since the incident in Paris before word of a new feat of the child again spread around the world.

It happened during the time of the disorders in Barcelona, when mounted carabineers were attacking a small group of workers. The crowd, however, contrary to custom, was not without arms. Volleys of shots came one after the other, and before anybody could understand what was happening, about forty carabineers were lying on the ground with their riderless horses galloping about in the square. Ten people in the crowd were armed with the new American pistols. Success intoxicates, and the crowd increased rapidly. Barricades were hastily erected; the authorities called out the infantry and artillery, and by nightfall managed to clear the streets. About one thousand people were killed or wounded.

The Spanish government forbade the import and sale of the automatic pistols. For a whole week the newspapers discussed the "revolution in Barcelona," and the orders arrived in such quantities that even Jones became nervous. The shares of the company rose sharply, and the financial genius spoke of a new issue and further expansion of the business.

But Hugh suddenly felt that none of this mattered any longer. One morning he woke up with one thought, one thought alone, in his mind: Madge!

By evening he was on his way to Los Angeles.

What transpired surprised Hugh. He imagined that the meeting with Madge would be different somehow. When the train at last arrived, he went straight from the station to find her. The aunt lived in a quiet street a good way from the center of town. Madge, dressed in black, had grown thin and looked like a young girl; she was sitting in the front room with two girls, reading aloud in French.

"It's me, Madge," said Hugh.

He knew perfectly well that it could not have been otherwise, but Madge's face was so unexpectedly familiar; it seemed extraordinary that this Madge was so like the one he knew.

They were barely able to exchange two words for the first hour. Hugh's arrival was a pleasant surprise for Madge and his news interested her, but she did not quite believe him and kept on her guard. Hugh was given to fantasies and could invent anything, but the important thing was that he had come. Madge began to feel very warm toward Hugh and had already decided that she would not let him go. But outwardly she was quietly sizing him up, wondering how best to conduct herself—women are always preoccupied with the effect they're making, except when they lose their temper. Hugh seemed to Madge as foolish as ever, but very nice. They had not seen each other for two years.

Eventually, Hugh discovered the right approach: he took Madge shopping, and they began to buy everything they saw—flowers, hats, silk stockings, diamonds, pearls, chocolates. Madge resisted for some time, but in the end her heart took over and she began to choose presents for her aunt, the aunt's children, and the servants. This finally melted the ice. They had lunch, went for a drive along the seashore, and then found themselves back at the shops. It was not until evening that Hugh remembered he had nowhere to stay, and telephoned to reserve the very biggest and costliest suite in the most luxurious hotel—eight rooms with a sea view, a Louis XV bedroom, a dining room like a Gothic church, a separate conservatory, marble baths in Roman style, and balconies facing the sea.

That night was a second honeymoon. Hugh would not hear of Madge returning to her aunt's. The aunt was somewhat scandalized by such an abduction, but Madge stayed.

For a long time they sat on the balcony, looking at the ocean, watching the stars beginning to appear.

"Two days ago I saw you in my dreams," said Madge. "Where were you then?"

"In the train," said Hugh, "somewhere near Chicago."

"Were you thinking about me?"

"What else could I have been thinking about?"

"Wicked Hugh, why did you write so rarely? No, the fault was mine! I should not have run away and left you. But I couldn't, Hugh darling, forgive me, I couldn't stay there. When I remember our apartment and you, always busy, gloomy, discontented, and the dreadful smell of that drink you were poisoning yourself with, I don't know what I might have done. But I do know that had I everything to do over again, I'd still run away. And I know that I am right. If all had come to nothing, you would have come here and we could have started working together. Ah, Hugh, you cannot imagine how good it is on a flower plantation. I still can't seem to believe in your millions yet; maybe it would have been better if you had come without them. You are somehow different."

Later they went indoors and looked around their apartment. They were slightly embarrassed by it; there was too much silk, bronze, marble, too many carpets and flowers.

By now both of them had begun to feel that they could not spend any more time apart. Madge felt guilty toward Hugh and Hugh felt guilty toward Madge. And everything happened as in a dream. They suddenly began to speak of everything and anything in the world and, as you might expect, their talk was interspersed with an abundance of kisses.

Hugh undressed Madge, kissed her shoulders, hands, feet, hair. He felt that he had been dead these last two years and was only now beginning to live.

"Hugh, you must forgive me," said Madge. "I cannot live without sun, without flowers, and without children. Those last years in New York were like being in prison. When you talked about Venice or some grand place we would go when we were rich, you didn't realize how awful you made me feel. I would have jumped out of the window —anything rather than listen! But I do see how you must have suffered, my poor darling. You believed in it all . . ."

"Hugh, you must give me your word," said Madge half an hour later.

"Anything, dearest."

"You see, I do believe you, but if everything had been different—no money, no invention, no riches—give me your word that you would give up inventing and work with me on a flower farm till we have saved enough money to buy a farm of our own. I have already thought it all out. We would first lease the land, then build the house . . . All right? When it is built, we would move in. I am good at rose-growing now. You cannot imagine how many kinds of roses there are, and how full of life they are, almost like children. All this, Hugh, if you were penniless. Hugh, will you give me your word?"

"Of course I will, darling."

And so on, and so forth. I omit the description of the wedding night, although it could be done very touchingly were one to relate everything this sweet couple said about children they would have. Madge wanted to have six children, a boy and a girl first, then two boys and then another two girls.

"One more," said Hugh.

"All right, a little tiny one," said Madge.

They were enjoying themselves on the whole, and this enraged me. You know I do not care for such moods. All these raptures, delights, reveries, hopes, engender in me a condition not unlike seasickness. But there was nothing I could do. All the same, in my heart of hearts I reckoned that in the end it might not turn out so perfectly.

The following day, when Hugh stepped out onto the side balcony, the cries of newspaper sellers reached him.

"Extra! Extra! Terrible robbery in San Diego! Twenty dead and wounded!"

When a Negro flunkey in a red tailcoat and white gaiters brought in the newspapers on a silver tray, Hugh read the headlines at a glance; they were printed across the whole width of the page: ROBBERY IN SAN DIEGO. TRAIN AMBUSH. TERRIBLE INCIDENT, RETURN OF THE SAVAGE WILD WEST. TWENTY DEAD AND WOUNDED. THREE NEWLY WED COUPLES AMONG THE DEAD. TWO BANDITS ARRESTED.

What had happened did indeed take one back to the days of the Wild West. Two men in black masks had blown up a tunnel and stopped a train filled with the early

spring tourists bound for the mountains. With a few shots
they finished off the driver and fireman, and then with cries
of "Hands up!" they began to drive the passengers out of
the coaches. Somebody fired a shot. The men started shooting into the crowd. Twenty people fell. Besides the three
couples eight men and six women had been shot and
wounded. The bandits disappeared, having seized about
forty thousand dollars in money and valuables. But, as the
newspaper reported, they had already been caught.

The terrible toll of casualties was explained by the
killers' formidable weapons, explained the newspapers:
each man had two pistols of the automatic type which, said
the report, represented the last word in guns.

"Well, I'm damned," said Hugh. But for some reason
he felt ill-at-ease. And he threw away the newspapers so
that Madge would not come across them.

LYNCH LAW IN MOUNTAINS! CRIMINALS EXECUTED
BY CITIZENS! printed the evening newspapers in huge letters.

A posse of hooded horsemen had apparently captured
the two train robbers from the sheriff and his deputies,
poured kerosene over them, and burned them alive.

Hugh was very glad that Madge had no interest in
newspapers.

They spent the day, as they themselves described it, in
fairyland. It was the day of white roses.

Madge began to feel like a millionairess and announced
that she wanted no other flowers but white roses.

The day of white roses became a week. Hugh had no
wish to leave sun-soaked Los Angeles with its glittering
ocean and blue mountains in the distance.

Years later they would remember this beginning of
their second honeymoon. But on the fifth day Jones called

Hugh back to New York with a veritable salvo of special telegrams. They had received a tremendous number of new orders, but it was necessary to decide on new financial policies. A trip to Europe was essential.

Hugh hired a coach on the trans-America express. Madge was still agitated by all the extravagance, but she was beginning to feel the pleasure of spending money without regard for expense, and when the train started, she cuddled up to Hugh and said, "Hugh, darling, say you won't ever leave me again."

"Of course I won't. Not ever, sweetheart," replied Hugh.

He felt triumphant and believed his greatest reward to be Madge herself. You people are unbelievably stupid!

Hugh arranged matters with the Belgian manufacturers very quickly and profitably. Then they went to Paris, and here Hugh's old dreams came true. There were evenings at the Paris opera, lunches in the Café Anglais, exhibitions where Hugh could buy pictures, race meetings where he could buy horses. But all this translated into reality seemed more like ordinary life and less like the fairyland it had seemed from a distance.

Hugh and Madge thought Paris rather dirty and very small. Each kept quiet, trying to hide his impressions from the other, but Madge inadvertently let it slip out on the return journey and both of them burst out laughing. Only much later did Hugh began to value Paris at its true worth.

When Hugh returned from Europe, it became apparent that the business needed further expansion. Orders continued to flood in. Requests for three and four years ahead came from Japan, Greece, South Africa.

The work had to be divided. Jones took over the factory, and Hugh, with the financial genius, the management side of the business. It became necessary to arrange matters so that the company could grow without hindrance to meet the increasing demand. Hugh found people. More accurately they found him, and together they succeeded in widening the joint-stock company, attracting huge capital to it, and buying up a number of factories, thus ensuring the production of pistols in quantities sufficient, they hoped, to satisfy demand. At this point, the enterprise was renamed the General Automatic Weapon Company. Work on production for Europe had already started in the Belgian factories.

But the incident with Mimi Lacertier upset all calculations and created such an increase in demand for pistols that Hugh and Jones again found themselves barely in command of the situation.

The Mimi Lacertier episode occurred about a year after the tragic death of Marion Gray, and once again in Paris.

Mimi Lacertier was in her second season as a Parisian celebrity. She could not, of course, be compared with Marion Gray. Even so, there was not a single person in Paris who did not know her name.

Mimi was a music-hall singer from Montmartre, and she had become famous by reason of her costume, which a well-known novelist had designed for her to wear at a certain literary cabaret. The costume was simple and original— a black mask, black corset, black stockings, and that was all. Mimi was a tall blonde with a pale body and golden hair. Her first appearance on stage in this costume created a furor. The public became wildly enthusiastic, roared and stamped, shouting her name; they refused to go home and eventually the police were forced to intervene. The night ended with Mimi's arrest. There was a trial. Mimi was fined and sentenced to a week in jail for offending public decency. As a protest against such injustice, a group of students and artists marched along the main avenue carrying portraits of Mimi Lacertier.

As soon as Mimi was released, she started appearing again in the same costume, only without the mask. And the corset was considerably reduced in length. In time, there was not a single urchin in Paris who did not know Mimi's song "Mon corset." And of course Mimi herself became the most fashionable and expensive lady in all gay Paris.

Everything was going perfectly; Mimi could have had a great future in financial and political spheres. She was, however, drawn to the bohemian world. At heart, she was a grisette of the old type, always in and out of love, madly jealous and possessive. Her latest lover was a rising young painter named Max, the owner of an exceptionally silky mustache and a very fickle heart. For him, Mimi discarded all other men. For his part, at the end of a fortnight, the artist dropped her in favor of Susanne Ivry.

Mimi wept and vowed she would enter a nunnery; instead, that night, feeling especially sad, she appeared on stage wearing nothing but a velvet ribbon around her throat. Then she went home. It was already morning.

She slept badly and awoke with a sallow face and a migraine. She seemed to be aware of every nerve in her body, almost as if she could hear them. The first thing she remembered was her faithless lover. She wanted to scream and weep. Lord, what would she not give to have Susanne Ivry run over by a coach or stricken with smallpox! But what would it be to him? In two weeks' time he would have someone new. Was there really nothing she could do to make him come back to her? To make him suffer, to make him beg for her love so that she could proudly refuse him? But Mimi felt that she would not be able to resist for long. That was the worst of it: men value only those women who make them suffer, and Mimi could never manage that when she was in love. But what was she to do?

Mimi felt that she simply could not leave the painter and Susanne Ivry in peace, as if everything was *comme il faut*. No, that just could not be!

She took a long time to dress, her thoughts preoccupied. Hazily, she imagined a scene; then the veil was drawn aside and she saw the course she must follow. When she left home she put the American pistol in her muff. It was terribly heavy. At the last minute Mimi wavered: should she take it or not? She was not at all sure that she would be able to do what she had in mind. But in the end she did . . . just in case she felt inclined to frighten Susanne and Max.

Movement was difficult at the bazaar. Sarah Bernhardt and other celebrities were serving, but even so, when Mimi approached, the crowd parted and all eyes followed her. She recognized the deputy who had vilified her in his speeches, and noticed in his quick glance a kind of suspicious curiosity. Mimi was amused. People around her were whispering. She heard only her own name. All her hostility seemed to dissipate.

But suddenly, not in the least as she had pictured it, Mimi saw Max and Susanne. They did not even acknowledge her. Susanne casually glanced her way, touched Max's hand, and drew his attention to a display on the right, as if something had taken her fancy. Max, at ease and unconcerned, looked Mimi's way, then turned back to Susanne with an affectionate smile.

The crowd separating them had passed, and Mimi, ablaze with rage, found herself face to face with the couple.

Still they ignored her presence. Susanne rather casually examined her, and Max gazed absent-mindedly over her head. This was intolerable to Mimi. Her nerves began to quiver, her head was in a whirl. She drew back and shrieked a Montmartre epithet. She saw Susanne flush with anger and Max turn pale. They were the center of all eyes. But there was no holding back now, she would do everything as planned. Triumphantly she took the American pistol from her muff and pointed it first at Max, then at Susanne. Just as she had imagined it, everything fell silent.

But then something terrible happened, something Mimi neither expected nor wanted.

The child had one embarrassing trait: it was inclined to start speaking before it was asked.

The pistol suddenly jerked up in Mimi's hand, a yellow spark flashed and there was a dreadful bang. Deadly terror gripped her. What had happened? She had not intended to shoot. She did not even know whether the terrible thing had been loaded. Her heart was throbbing wildly in her breast; her head was swimming. Mimi wanted to shriek that it was all wrong, that she had not wanted this, but she could not speak.

A tall gentleman with a black beard raised his stick and rushed toward her. Instinctively, Mimi raised the pistol. The pistol jerked, again the yellow spark flashed and the dreadful bang exploded. Mimi longed to flee from it all, but her legs would not obey her. The tall gentleman with the beard was crawling about on hands and knees. Somewhere far away the crowd was screaming. The scene spun before Mimi's eyes and as the shrieks of the crowd grew nearer and shriller, she feared that in another moment the mob would throw itself upon her and tear her to pieces for what she had done. Mimi screamed, closed her eyes, lifted the pistol. Again the dreadful bang, a scream, another bang, another and another! Then no more. Mimi dropped the child and collapsed beside it.

You can imagine what happens at a fashionable charity bazaar when someone starts shooting nickel-cased bullets into the crowd. When the first shot was heard there was a shout of "Anarchists!" and everyone rushed for the doors. For ten minutes pandemonium reigned.

This was a sight worth seeing, I can tell you. About forty people were crushed to death, mainly women, and twice as many were injured. (And such injuries!) The faces of those elegant women were disfigured, their teeth were knocked out, jawbones dislocated, their hair clawed out. A sight indeed! And this was a high-society occasion!

When the guards eventually reached Mimi, they found her on the floor with her mouth open and her eyes glazed. She died not long afterwards of a ruptured heart. Susanne was killed on the spot, three more were killed, and several wounded.

SCENES FROM DANTE'S HELL AT CHARITY BAZAAR! wrote the newspapers. MORE THAN A HUNDRED VICTIMS! SAVAGE BEAST AWAKENS IN PEOPLE OF CULTURE!

After this, there was not a single decent apache in Paris, not one self-respecting safebreaker, not one anarchist of any standing who did not hurry to acquire the flat black pistol, inconspicuous in the pocket and infallible in times of trouble. The advantages of the child were obvious, and its only shortcoming was that it sometimes spoke several seconds before it was asked. From my point of view, this was a merit, for it made for more animated conversation.

Paris led the other capitals of Europe. The provinces did not want to lag behind the capitals. Small countries hurried to catch up with the big ones. To east, south, west, and north, the child was in equal demand.

People who tired of their own lives; people who felt hampered by those nearest and dearest to them; people whose lives were threatened by those closest to them—all acquired the child. It became somehow a universal trump in the game of life. With it, it seemed, it was easy enough to win or (if one wanted) to lose.

Depression, despair, grief, hate, envy, jealousy, greed, cowardice, anger, cruelty, unfaithfulness, treachery, and scores of related emotions, with the help of the child achieved their very best and fullest expression. The child was there where life had begun to overflow its ordinary narrow and vulgar channels. Every report of a more or less conspicuous crime—assassination, robbery with murder, sensational suicides—invariably carried mention of the child's name. It was considered well-nigh indecent to undertake something serious with the old revolver—rather like using a bow and arrow.

The world expressed the greatest possible interest in Hugh's invention. It would not be exaggerating to say that the distribution of pistols manufactured by the General Automatic Weapon Company far exceeded that of the Bible. But this was only the beginning.

At approximately the time of the tragic case of Mimi Lacertier, Madge had her first child.

In Hugh and Madge's life, as I have already told you, the decision not to have children had played a very special part. But when the success of Hugh's invention made it possible for them to meet again and renew their love for each other, they quickly changed their minds. The realization that they could now have children transformed their love for one another and they discovered an enchantment they had not known before.

When it was certain that Madge was going to become a mother, Hugh felt as though she had been elevated to some inaccessible regal height. He seemed to see her for the first time, so mysterious, secretive, and coolly detached had she become.

He felt the urge to create appropriate surroundings for the arrival of their first-born.

But here Hugh suffered an early setback. He could never catch up with the growth of his income. Everything he started to establish for himself very soon seemed small and poor in comparison with the visions made possible by his increasing income. The house Hugh had built himself by the factory seemed miserable and vulgar after only six months in it. Another house which he had started building in New York he left unfinished to build a new one in the middle of a vast piece of land bought at an extravagant price from a ruined millionaire.

This house was not ready when Madge had her first child. So, in honor of the birth, Hugh canceled all past plans and projects and announced a competition for a mansion, with a huge prize for the winning design.

Madge liked the magnificence of their new life. She wished only that Hugh could have more time with her. He was much too busy, forever immersed in new financial projects, or traveling to Paris or Rio de Janeiro, or somewhere. Madge saw him seldom at this time.

Hugh himself noticed that his new status bore little resemblance to his dreams of the past. His dreams of visiting Italy to enjoy the marvels of nature and art at leisure; tranquil, unhurried travels in the Orient, to Jerusalem and Cairo—these were now probably even less possible than at the time Hugh worked as a draftsman. But Hugh did not give up hoping. The important thing now was that his family life and his relationship with Madge were exceptionally fulfilling, his whole being seemed permeated by her radiance. From the time of the birth of her first child, Madge did indeed seem to possess an inner light felt by all around her.

Another year or two passed thus. The mansion, designed by an Italian architect, was nearly ready. Madge was expecting her second child, and the General Automatic Weapon Company had been so successful that Hugh's name now appeared in newspapers beside that of Vanderbilt, Astor, and Rockefeller.

Hugh found he had acquired a number of relatives. One of them had even written a book about their genealogy. Reviewing the book, the newspapers had written that Hugh represented the real aristocracy of the United States, as a descendant of the pioneers who had carried the banner of the white man's culture, and so on and so forth. One of the large illustrated monthlies featured a detailed biography of one of Hugh's ancestors, the one who had been Governor of South Carolina; the text was interspersed with numerous drawings and photographs of old engravings. One well-known English historian had written to Hugh, saying that he had found unquestionable proof of his descent from King Arthur and asked only a hundred thousand pounds for further research and the printing of his findings.

The great epoch of wars had begun.

Wars, which had formerly occurred at intervals of several decades, now followed each other without a break. And all these wars, slaughters, revolutions, massacres were preceded and accompanied by colossal orders for the article manufactured by the company.

All this made me very glad. I like people, as you know, and wish them the very best, and such a livening-up of the political scene pointed to an uncommonly rapid growth of culture. It has long been known that war is the highest expression of civilization and progress. What would have happened to people if there had been no war? Savagery, barbarism, and a complete absence of evolution. It has always seemed to me, though, that the importance of wars in the political and moral development of man has never been sufficiently appreciated. People have been talking far too much about everlasting peace just recently.

Dreams of peace make even the most civilized nations anemic and generally indicate that the country is at a low ebb. On the whole, only the tired, exhausted, and spiritually deprived indulge in dreams of everlasting peace. War is the creative principle of the world. Without war, unhealthy developments begin to appear—mysticism, erotica, decadence in art, and a general decline of the healthy and the strong. Long periods of peace always lead to degeneration.

"You are astonished that I speak thus? It is my firm conviction," said the Devil with a wave of his tail. "War is a moral necessity. Idealism demands war. Only materialism balks at it, because war teaches, not with sermons, but in practice, how very transient are all the blessings of this world, how very unstable is everything terrestrial and temporal."

And so, accordingly, I could do no more than welcome the beginning of continuous war.

The future prosperity of the company seemed to be assured.

In addition to pistols, the factories had for some time been manufacturing automatic rifles. But demand for them so far came only from South America.

"Mark my words," Jones would say, "in ten or fifteen years all Europe will be rearming with automatic rifles. At present it's simply that no one dares to be first."

"Yes, maybe you are right," Hugh would say. "But whether that's true or not, we must think in terms of a big expansion of the business."

"That's certain," Jones would answer. "We must build without a break. What I would like is a small artillery section. You know we have a project for a remarkable rapid-firing three-incher in the works."

"That's true," said Hugh. "But we must wait for the results of the experiments with the new kinds of gunpowder and explosives. I have ten people on this project. I find the experiments with explosives which affect the eyes particularly interesting. The rabbits and dogs have gone blind beautifully, and we have now begun experiments on horses."

"All right," said Jones. "We will wait; but all the same we must not put it off for long."

By now the factories occupied and supported an entire town. Hugh and Jones gave a great deal of attention to the planning and organization of this town and were extremely proud that their workers had the lowest mortality rate in the United States.

The workers' houses stood amidst gardens; fields and groves surrounded the schools, churches, and houses. All workers who served a certain length of time received pensions, and a six-hour working day was introduced as an experiment.

Both Hugh and Madge gave much of their time to the needs of the factory housing estate. Madge always said that the greatest delight of her life was to make all these people as contented and happy as possible.

But Hugh could never completely conquer his slight feeling of contempt for the workers. He did everything in his power for them, but he could never acknowledge them as his equals. He respected only those who could and would not be enslaved.

Hugh's dearest creation was his Institute for the Promotion of Young Inventors. It began as follows:

Some five years after the change in his circumstances, Hugh came across an address he had written in an old notebook. He prided himself on his memory, but now, no matter how he racked his brains, he could not remember who Anthony Seymour was. Then he suddenly remembered his meeting in Central Park with the pathetic old inventor. That had been one of the most desperate days of his life. Hugh recalled that he had promised that he would seek out this man on the day his fortunes took a turn for the better, and felt ashamed that he had forgotten. Besides, he had of late been mulling over the idea that something should be done for people in his former condition.

Hugh instructed his lawyer to find Anthony Seymour, the inventor, who had given his address care of some tobacconist five years previously. Of course, neither Seymour nor the shop was to be found. All inquiries came to nothing. Hugh was very disappointed when in the end not even a trace of Anthony Seymour could be found.

This was the goad Hugh needed to set up his institute, which he opened a year later. Hugh found several young assistants who were keen on the idea, put large funds at their disposal, and the new institute began to function.

Hugh's idea was to help people of above-average ability to gain the status in life they deserved.

"The terrifying flaw in our society," Hugh said to his assistants, "is that everything is geared to the lowest common denominator. Schools, institutions, political parties, all have the lower type of person in mind. Theoretically, they are adapted to the middle level, but in practice they serve the lower. Socialism also aims at this level. We must aim at the highest. Never think of the word 'inventor' in its narrow sense: any person who has an idea of his own is an inventor."

Hugh's idea did not bear fruit immediately. The first collection of geniuses discovered by the institute proved in the main to be either charlatans or psychopaths. But after a time people of genuine worth began to appear, and from time to time a real original would turn up among them, and in ten years Hugh's institute was known throughout the globe. Without doubt, mankind is indebted to Hugh for the preservation of many valuable discoveries which might otherwise have been lost for good.

It was one of the institute inventors who should take credit for the principle of the rapid-firing gun of which Jones had spoken. And it was a group of young chemists from the same establishment who were entrusted with certain problems regarding new kinds of gunpowder and new explosives using poisonous gases.

The expanding business of the General Automatic Weapon Company meant the establishment of a number of peripheral enterprises. It soon became evident that it was more profitable for the company to run its own iron and copper mines, coal pits, and oil wells. Then the Company had to build some thousand miles of railways, absorbing as it did so several neighboring lines which had been unable to withstand competition. Then Jones (who in general showed little interest in the financial side) made a very profitable take-over of a shipping company, and the General Company found itself with a fleet of forty ocean-going steamers.

But all this did not now have an absolute claim on Hugh's and Jones's time. Much of what they had previously had to do was now done for them; besides, the business developed by itself—capital, profits, and the various branches of the business flourished independently.

At last Hugh could travel. With Madge or alone he traveled to Europe, Asia, Africa, South America. And often, sitting in his New York palace, closing his eyes, and going over his travels in his mind, he thought how it had all enriched his soul.

An interest in art, which Hugh developed after several journeys to Italy, filled his life with new meaning. He began to buy numbers of pictures, and, though it may seem strange in a person untutored in art, he bought well from the outset. In a few years he had succeeded in assembling a fascinating collection of paintings by contemporary artists of the new schools.

But, as he said himself, his deepest feeling was reserved for works of art which stayed in the place where they had been conceived and created. Because of this, he found collections gathered and brought to America strangely lifeless. During his travels in Italy and Spain he would walk into an ancient little church in an out-of-the-way hamlet and suddenly sense a strange and inexplicable joy; from some distant depth of his soul, voices would sound, awakened by the face of a Madonna standing against a dark background, or in the gloom and silence of the high vault by a ray of the evening sun penetrating the stained glass, or by the dull echo of steps on the stone slabs.

And then Hugh was aware of the secret essences which lived and moved in all that surrounded him, embodied in the paintings of the old masters, in ancient churches, walls, and turrets, but always at one with the countryside from which they arose—the vineyard on the hill, the setting sun, the yellow stone road, the chain of hills on the horizon.

Such were Hugh's most treasured experiences, following which ordinary everyday life seemed faded, strange, and unreal.

Hugh's next passion was astronomy.

He had been sailing in his huge yacht to the estuary of the Amazon. It was evening. Madge and the children had gone below and Hugh went up on the bridge. It was a warm and dark tropical night, humid and full of glittering stars. Hugh gazed at the sky for a long time. And suddenly he remembered how keen he had been on astronomy in his early youth.

"All that I had to abandon at the time," he said to himself. "But now . . . why should I not take it up now? Who was it who spoke about the starry sky and the soul of man?"

Hugh considered how the stars attracted him, how the mere contemplation of the incredible distances between the stars and the earth could cause everything earthbound to diminish and depart from him. His being was roused.

He did not leave the bridge until late that night, and the very next day took over all the books on astronomy which the captain happened to have with him, in addition to his globe and various charts of the stars.

For the remainder of the cruise Hugh thought of nothing but stars. And when he returned to New York, he felt he had become another person. The stars had taken him away from the desert of business in which he had been languishing for the last few years. He became the Hugh of old, dreamer of the impossible, giving free rein to his soaring imagination.

In New York he began to assemble a library on astronomy and set up a small observatory which cost about a million dollars. He invited a young scientist to take charge and was himself so taken with it that he spent whole days and nights there. Here Hugh really found himself. He had noted with surprise that his gift for invention seemed to have abandoned him of late. But now it returned in double and treble strength. Now he worked for the sake of knowledge alone, creative work, winning over and extorting from nature her closest secrets. His dream was to communicate with other planets; his plans progressed.

·   ·   ·

During the very first year of his new life, Hugh started building greenhouses for Madge. In time these became a botanical garden under glass where only roses were cultivated, but roses of all kinds. The roses were Madge's pride and joy. On the birthday of her first child, Hugh Jr., she always had a tea party in the rose gallery, regularly reported by the New York press.

Madge also had philanthropic inclinations and was building a garden city for the blind.

Hugh and his family regularly spent the month of August in his mountain retreat, not far from New York. At the time of which I speak, his eldest son had just returned from Paris, where he was studying mathematics and astronomy; his two daughters, both of whom were greatly interested in painting, had come back from Japan; and the youngest son, who had an exceptional talent for music, was convalescing from severe influenza.

Hugh was extremely proud of his children. But he always called them "Madge's children," acknowledging her prior claim to them, for they had been in her thoughts and dreams long before they had actually come to be.

When the whole family had gathered, Madge went away for several days to see how the building of her garden city was progressing. Shortly before she was due to return, a telegram arrived from her saying: "At last, it has been possible for me too to make if not an invention then a discovery. Will tell you on return."

On the way home from the station, Madge refused to talk about her "invention" and said that it should wait until the evening.

After dinner they drank coffee on the wide verandah overlooking a deep valley, beyond which were hills covered with fir trees, and two waterfalls just visible in the blue distance. For some two years now Madge had held this place dearer even than her rose plantations in California.

"How terrible it must be to live in darkness and not be able to see the sun, mountains, the green . . . think of it, children," said Madge. "I cannot think of anything worse. And that is why I have been so happy these last few days. I can do more for the blind than I thought. I wanted only to alleviate their lot, and now it seems possible that we can treat many who have been regarded as hopeless cases. I have found a remarkable doctor who treats the blind by suggestion under hypnosis. What I have seen is like a miracle. Real healing of the blind. I saw myself how a person after being blind for ten years *began to see*. Even those born blind sometimes respond to this treatment. This doctor of mine says that nearly ten percent of those regarded as permanently blind are not incurable at all. He says that until hypnotism has been tried, one cannot properly speak of *blindness*. In his opinion, ordinary doctors do a lot of damage telling patients that there is no hope for them. As a result, the patients actually go blind, mainly through auto-suggestion. The eye is such a delicate organ that it is sensitive to every suggestion. So you see, if under hypnosis one suggests a reversal by commanding the eyes to see, they obey and begin to see, except where the nerve is atrophied. But this doctor is not given a chance. The eye doctors in New York forbade him to experiment in eye hospitals, and this after he had cured a girl born blind. Just think, isn't it dreadful? These eye doctors are themselves stone-blind! So I have decided to build a clinic for this doctor near my garden city and to found an institute where young doctors can learn the new method. Think how much good can be done, and what a joy it is to have the opportunity to do good!"

"Well, you know," said the Devil, "all this was so beautiful that I just could not sit it out any longer. I have already told you that sentimentality has the same effect on me as rough seas on a human being prone to seasickness. I took my leave, and what it was they went on to talk about, I do not know."

"But in the final account," said I, "what does it all mean —was it right or wrong? Was it necessary for Hugh to strive to become an inventor or would it have been better to stay put like everybody else? I do not understand."

The Devil flared up in an angry green flame and banged his fist down on the table with a shattering blow.

"I told you not to ask for a moral!" he roared. "Make of it what you will! Just leave me in peace! As if I could begin to understand the first thing about you people!"

And he vanished beneath the earth, leaving behind only an odor of sulfur.

The Devil has become terribly irritable of late.

THE BENEVOLENT DEVIL

It happened when I was traveling in India.

One morning I found myself in Ellora, where the famous cave temples are.

You have no doubt read or heard about this place.

The mountain range runs from Daulatabad and is cut by sharp ridges and deep valleys enclosing the ruins of dead towns; it ends in a sheer rock ledge, horseshoe-shaped and several miles long. Stretching up from the ravine is a concave wall pitted with holes like huge swallows' nests—these are the openings of the cave temples. The whole rock face is pierced with temples penetrating deep into the earth. There are fifty-eight temples here, all belonging to different ancient religions and different gods, each one superseding the last.

Inside the huge dark halls, at a height unpenetrated by the light of torches, one can hear the rustling of scores of bats. Here are long corridors, narrow passages, inner courtyards; unexpected balconies and galleries with a view of the plains below; slippery staircases polished by bare feet thousands of years ago; dark wells beyond which one can sense hidden caves; twilight, silence undisturbed by a single sound. Bas-reliefs and statues of many-armed and many-headed gods; most of all, the god Shiva—dancing, killing, and merging in convulsive embrace with other figures.

Shiva is the god of Love and Death, with whose strange, cruel, and strongly erotic cult is connected the most idealistic and abstract system of Indian philosophy. Shiva, the dancing god around whom the whole universe dances as his radiant reflection. All contradictions blend in a mysterious way in this god of a thousand names. Shiva, the benevolent and merciful, the deliverer from misfortune, the divine healer, with a thousand eyes and a thousand quivers of arrows to vanquish demons. Shiva, protector of "the human herd," with throat blue from a poison intended to annihilate mankind, which he drank himself in order to save the human race. Shiva, "the great time," continuous renewer of all he has destroyed. In this sense he is represented as a lingam, a black phallus existing in the ether, and worshipped as the source of life and god of voluptuousness. Equally he is Shiva the god of asceticism and ascetics, himself the great ascetic "clothed in air"; the god of wisdom, god of cognition and light. He is also the lord of evil, who lives in cemeteries and crematoria and wears a crown of snakes and a necklace of skulls. Shiva is at once god, priest, and sacrifice, *which is the whole universe.* The consort of Shiva is as mysterious and contradictory as he. She has many different faces and is known by a variety of names: Parvati, goddess of beauty, love, and happiness; Durga, patroness of mothers and family; and Kali, the black one, mistress of cemeteries, dancer among ghosts, goddess of evil, disease, murder, and simultaneously goddess of wisdom and revelation.

Further along the rock face are the temples of Buddha, where men have renounced the world and prayed for deliverance from it; these are places whose huge statues have stood silent and lost in contemplation for two thousand years.

In the center of the long chain of temples is the vast Kailas temple, or Temple of the Sky. Kailas is a mythical mountain in the Himalayas where the gods live—an Indian Olympus. A huge cavity was hollowed out of the rock for this temple. In the middle of the hollow stand three large pagodas decorated with carved-stone tracery; not a single stone is laid upon another—all is hewn out of solid rock. Two gigantic statues of elephants, several times their natural size, stand at the sides of the pagodas, also hewn from the stone. Fanning out and boring deep into the rock behind are galleries, underground passages, and dark, mysterious halls, whose rough walls still bear marks of the instruments that chipped the granite; statues and bas-reliefs of terrifying gods stand in the recesses.

Once all this was full of life. There were moving crowds of pilgrims thronging to the festivities on nights of the full moon, to watch the sacred dances and to make sacrifices; hundreds of lithe dancers flitted about, the scent of jasmine was everywhere. In the inner sanctum the magic rites of mysterious cults were performed. Some say traces of these rites still survive in India today, though they are carefully concealed from Europeans. All the caves, down to the very depths, once had a life of their own, a life we cannot even begin to understand.

Nowadays nothing of this is to be seen. The city of temples is a wilderness. There are no Brahmin priests, no dancers, no wandering fakirs, no pilgrims; no more are the endless processions of elephants, nobody brings flowers, no one lights the fires. As far as the eye can see, there is not a single village or a sign of life across the plains below. Only in two or three hamlets, hidden in the trees, live a few watchmen who act as guides.

The caves and the temples appear as in a dream. Nowhere in the world does reality blend with the dream world so completely as in these caves. Everyone entering them shares the vague recollection of walking in a dream through dark corridors and narrow passages like these; of climbing, terrified of falling, up steep and slippery steps; of bending down and putting a hand out to feel the uneven walls and floor; of passing through narrow slanting galleries and emerging on the slope of the rock, where far down below stretches the misty plain. Perhaps none of this happened; perhaps it did. But the memory of the dark corridors and galleries lingers.

It was summer—the rainy season. The plains below were covered with a thick green carpet, and everywhere brooks burbled over rocks to mingle with others further down and obstruct the route to the distant caves.

Starting early in the morning, I spent the whole day roaming about the temples with a camera, going down into the caves, climbing over rocks, scrambling up to the top of the slope, and always returning to the temples. All this I did with a kind of eager, avid curiosity, as if I knew or sensed somehow that it was here, in this very place, that I would find something I had been searching for. Several times I went right down onto the plains, which were overgrown with vegetation and saturated with water, and tried separate approaches to the most remote and inaccessible part of the temple-city. I had been told that there was here, in the third or fourth temple from the end, a certain bas-relief, or symbolic wall drawing, and I was determined to find it, and if possible, photograph it. My guides diligently searched for a way through, wading waist-deep in the bubbling, muddy streams, splashing fearlessly through the wet, snake-infested grass, and tearing a path through the dense bushes. But every time we came up against some obstacle—a steep rock face or deep water. It proved impossible to reach the right end of the horseshoe ledge by a shortcut from the plain. It had been raining all day with hardly a lull; now and again there was a downpour. At such times I took refuge in the nearest temple, lit a cigarette, and waited under a statue of the Buddha with the lowered eyes until the pelting torrents lessened to the familiar steady drizzle. All day long I did not see a single living thing, except my two guides (to whom I spoke in sign language, for they did not know a word of English), the bats in the caves, and the occasional gray hare starting from a bush as we approached.

In the end I lost hope of reaching the far temples from below, and decided that early the next day I would go straight along the top of the slope and try to reach them from above.

Toward evening, tired, hungry, and wet, I returned to the guesthouse.

This "rest-house" or "dawk-bungalow," of a kind to be found all over India, was about two miles from the caves, on a mountain slope in the vicinity of the crumbling tombs of the Muslim conquerors who had ravaged half of India in the seventeenth century.

It was already dark. I was so tired I could not eat, and went straight to bed. Evening parties are not the custom in India, and with the fall of dusk there is nothing left to do but go to bed.

The weather got worse. The monsoon was breaking. Sudden gusts of wind shook the whole house, and when the wind dropped, I could hear sheets of rain thundering on the roof. I desperately wanted to drop off to sleep quickly and get a good night's rest so that I could make an early start. Tomorrow I simply had to find that temple with the symbolic bas-relief on the wall. But for a long time I lay awake in a kind of heavy stupor, spellbound by the memory of the awe-inspiring temples, feeling that I wandered there still, gazing at the gods and wondering about the underground passages which connected the temples.

At the same time I found myself progressively gripped by a strange agitation. There was something terrifying in the incessant noise of rain and wind, which carried other unexpected sounds with it—the rattle of a train, although the railway was more than twenty miles away, or people's voices and the clatter of hooves on stones; then tramping, the measured steps of soldiers marching and the drone of singing, seeming sometimes nearer, sometimes farther away, but never for a moment ceasing.

Weariness took its toll on my nerves. I began to feel that something uncanny and hostile was surrounding me in this "dawk-bungalow." Somebody was watching me, somebody was stealthily approaching the small house. I knew that I was completely alone in it, that the doors were inadequately locked, and that the watchmen slept in their own hut at the other end of a large clearing.

This feeling of unease increased steadily and would not allow me to fall asleep. I began to be irritated, with myself, with the monsoon, with India, and with everything around. At the same time I was becoming more and more gripped by fear, as if I had come to a place of no return, where dangers loomed from all sides and something threatened from every corner. I found myself deciding that I would go no further the following day, but travel back to Daulatabad first thing in the morning. At this point, it seemed that my consciousness began to fade, and rows of images, pictures, and faces began to file before my eyes.

Suddenly something banged violently on the verandah a room away from me. At once all sleep was gone. The

now-familiar terror and the dread of some hostile and unpleasant presence gripped me with renewed force. I jumped
out of bed, took my revolver out of my suitcase, loaded it,
and put it on the table by my bed. For a time it seemed that
everything was calming down, and I dozed off.

I woke up with a jolt, and sat bolt upright. Someone
was knocking on my door, not with the usual light tapping
but gripping the handle of the door with both hands, furiously pulling and banging at it. Slowly, as if afraid to reveal that I was awake, I stretched out my hand and fumbled
for my revolver. Not until I had found it and aimed it at
the door did a singularly calm and sober-minded voice tell
me that it was only the wind knocking. Somewhat ashamed
of my actions, I put the revolver back and returned to bed.

The knocking ceased; but two rooms away from me a
door banged loudly shut, as if, despairing of making himself heard by me, somebody had gone out onto the verandah and slammed the door.

The "house for visitors" consisted of four rooms, two
of which faced a big verandah. All the rooms were linked
by doors. In my room were four doors, two opening into
the adjoining rooms and two leading outside.

For a while everything was silent, except for the pour-
ing rain. Then came again the loud banging of a door, and
in the next room a window frame rattled as though a fist
struck it. After several moments of silence, somebody or
something must have crept stealthily up and gripped the
handle of my door again, for it suddenly rattled furiously.

I could stand it no longer. I leaped out of bed, rushed
to the door, and flung it open. Beyond was darkness, and on
the left, a room away, a door banged. I returned to my
room, lit a candle, and inspected the doors and windows.
They were all cracked with the heat of the dry weather and
the bolts broken and useless. So long as I walked through

the house with the candle, all was quiet, and the doors seemed shut tight. But as soon as I returned, lay down, and put out the light, a door in the farthest room banged and the windows rattled. I recalled that I had not found any banging door, and began to wonder. My anxiety and alarm increased as I realized that sleep had gone completely, and that I would probably have to suffer this torment for the rest of the night. It was so absurd not to be able to fall asleep after such a day. I had not slept the night before, because I had had to change trains in the middle of the night. Early in the morning I had arrived in Daulatabad and dozed off for two hours in a guesthouse like the one I was in. Then, when the horses arrived, I had been jolted about for three hours in the wind and rain in a two-wheeled "tonga," pulled from hill to hill past fantastic ruins of fortresses and towns; and afterwards I had roamed among the caves from noon until dusk.

And now these accursed doors and this unaccountable, nameless fear drove away my sleep. Doing without sleep in India is doubly wearying, as the resulting exhaustion is harder to shake off than in other places. A trace of it will remain in the shape of apathy, indifference, irritability, and a complete absence of interest in anything. All this I knew from experience. Now I began to worry that tomorrow I would not want to go anywhere and nothing would interest me; and this realization irritated me still more.

Of all the problems of traveling, the most trying is lack of sleep. All the rest are bearable, but when sleep is impossible, one is overcome by a feeling of disintegration and one's normal self is transformed into a tired, capricious, irritable, and listless creature. This I dreaded most of all.

I call this "immersion in matter." Everything becomes flat, ordinary, prosaic; the voice of the mysterious and miraculous, which is so strongly heard in India, falls silent and seems no more than a foolish invention. You notice only the discomforts—the ridiculous and unpleasant side of everything and everybody. The mirror loses its luster and the world seems universally gray and flat.

This was what tomorrow promised in place of the awesome and unexpected visions which had struck me with such force in the caves the day before.

It seemed impossible to get back to sleep. At times the whole bungalow came to life as if it wanted to take off, and all the doors, windows, and shutters clattered simultaneously.

Gradually the feeling of terror and fear began to fade, probably from no more than exhaustion. Of course, under cover of this rattling and noise, anyone could have broken in. In the end, though, it was all the same to me: he who wants to, let him come in; I only want to sleep.

Then began a painful struggle. I tried every trick I knew to get to sleep. I tried relaxing all my muscles, letting my mind go blank; I listened to my heartbeat and tried to abandon myself to the rhythmic rocking of the waves which were running through my body. With closed eyes I attempted to penetrate the darkness and mark a central point into which I tried to sink by thinking of nothing. I succeeded in doing it more easily than usual. I did not have any intrusive thoughts and I went to sleep without difficulty. But as soon as my consciousness began to fade and dreams to appear, somebody started tearing at my door and banging on the verandah again. This noise penetrated my sleep and dragged me back.

For a while, during the brief moments of quiet between the paroxysms of rattling, I must have dropped off, only to wake up, concentrate again, and once more sink into sleep.

Then I remember wanting to get up one more time to try to fasten the shutters on the verandah; the fear seemed to have gone completely now. I thought how good it would be suddenly to find myself in the caves at night. Again the doors rattled and somebody paced the verandah. But nothing mattered to me any more . . . Pictures drifted into my mind, somebody was speaking right by my ear . . .

Now I saw that I was walking along the edge of the precipice above the temple of Kailas. Pagodas of stone, three in a row, stood below. I looked down, and then, thrusting slightly with my feet, I left the edge of the rock and began calmly and smoothly to fly over the pagodas. "This is far more comfortable," I said to myself, "than the roundabout way." I flew past the pagodas and landed on the ground, not far from the entrance.

I sat on the steps of the first pagoda, near the stone elephant with the broken-off trunk, and waited for somebody.

How strange, how could I forget! Of course, I was waiting for the Devil. Last time I saw him, we agreed to meet just here in the temple of Kailas. That was why I had come, although I had forgotten this on my way here.

The Devil came out from behind the elephant, wrapped in his black cloak, looking as if his presence was nothing out of the ordinary. He sat down on the pedestal of the elephant and leaned against one of the front legs.

"Well then, here I am," he said. "Now we can continue our talk."

As soon as he had said this, I remembered that he had promised to tell me, in detail, about devils, about their life and their role in human affairs. How could I have forgotten? Eagerly I prepared to listen. Meetings with the Devil and talks with him always showed things in a new and unexpected light, even things I thought I knew all about.

"I will repeat what I have said before," said the Devil. "You are interested in the nature of the satanic world and our relations with you humans. I told you at the time that you do not understand us and paint a completely false picture of the relationship. People make a great mistake when they think we cause them harm and evil. This is quite untrue. We are very distressed that people do not understand what we do for them. They do not know, indeed they never even imagine, that our whole life consists of constant sacrifice on behalf of the human race, whom we love, whom we serve, and without whom we cannot live."*

"Cannot live?"

"Yes, generally speaking, you have difficulty in understanding us, and it is difficult, first of all, because even if you do acknowledge us you regard us as creatures from some other world. Ha, ha, ha!" the Devil rocked with laughter. "Are we indeed! Creatures from another world! If only you knew how silly that sounds. We are the very quintessence of this world, the earth, matter. Do you understand? We form the bond, as it were, between you and the earth. And we make sure that this bond is not broken."

"You are called spirits of evil!"

"What nonsense! We are spirits of matter. What you call evil is, from our point of view, truth. It is often useful as a preliminary measure for binding you to the earth and preventing you from leaving it. All the same, to call us the spirits of evil is not correct. True, there are spirits of evil

---

* After this was written, a plagiarism on the part of the Devil was pointed out to me, which I myself had not noticed. He told me the very thing the devil said to Ivan Karamazov. ("I sincerely love people, but I have been slandered many times.") In connection with this, I can say that the coincidence is solely in this phrase. What the Devil says in everything else, bears no resemblance whatsoever to what is said by Dostoyevsky's devil. On the other hand, an inclination toward plagiarism is one of the basic traits in the character of a devil. Furthermore, I cannot represent him to myself entirely without plagiarism. *Author.*

among us, those like myself, for example. However, they are the exception. After all, even I am not nearly as powerful in this sphere as I am reputed to be. I do not produce evil, I only, so to speak, collect it. I am not a professional, only an amateur, a collector. There you are; very probably my inclinations are somewhat perverted. I am extremely fond of observing the way people perform their nasty deeds, especially if they use fine words at the same time. Unfortunately, it is very seldom that I can help them. You can see, from what I told you last time, that I am completely powerless in the most interesting cases. More often than not, you people have very peculiar ways. Therefore, I repeat, I am an exception. A large majority of our fraternity is thoroughly attached to people. But you do not understand what we are doing for you. Were it not for us, you would have been lost without trace, long ago."

"What would have happened to us without you?"

"You would have vanished, been completely annihilated, and dissolved in the cosmic ether," said the Devil, "just as you disappear when . . . when various foolish fantasies occur to you." He paused. "Such as that known as 'transferring consciousness into the other world.'

"You must remember from our former talks that I have not the faintest belief in other worlds; I consider them to be figments of the imagination. Consequently, I cannot give you any information about them. I know only those regions with which I have immediate contact, and for those with which I have no contact I do not admit existence. Do you understand? It means that people who go away from earth or lose contact with it are annihilated; they cease to exist anywhere at any time. So we pity you. What a shame you are so stupid, so susceptible to fantasies which bring ruin upon you. We try to do our best to keep you on earth. Had we not cared for you, you would have ceased to exist here long ago. As to where you would be—how should I know? To my way of thinking, nowhere, because to me there is nothing besides this world. We alone and only we keep you on this beautiful earth, give you the chance of admiring the sunset or the rising moon, listening to nightingales, loving, experiencing joy. Without us nothing would have been left of you."

"But wait," I said, "you just said yourself that you do not know where we would have been without you. Perhaps we might not have disappeared entirely, might not have annihilated ourselves, might not have ceased to exist anywhere anytime, as you said. Maybe, on the contrary, we might have started a new and far more pleasant life somewhere you did not exist. You know, of course, that such a theory exists."

"That's all a lot of nonsense. First of all, where is this somewhere? Where is it, on the right, on the left, in the east, in the west? It is a myth! And secondly, how are you going to enjoy something outside matter? All your pleasures are material, your bodies are matter, and without a material body you cannot experience sensation of any kind! He who is without sensations has no existence. Finally, even if you did enjoy yourselves there, without us, what satisfaction is this for us? What concern then would your pleasures be to us? I am telling you, we love you. Well, think for yourself: imagine a woman loves a man and you try to convince her that he would be far better off where she can never see him again. How do you think she will answer you? Do you think she will agree to let him go? Nothing in the world would persuade her, if she is a real, live woman. She will say: 'Even if it is not quite perfect for him here, he's got me here, and I will not let him go.' Isn't that true? And she will be right! You people are a funny lot, you understand perfectly, but still you ask us to do the impossible.

"Listen, is it really possible to believe in all these ravings about some world beyond? We know very well what happens to a human being when he dies. And we know perfectly well that he has in him nothing other than what has been put in by outside impressions. I am a positivist, or to be more precise, a monist. I acknowledge only one beginning of the universe, by which a visible, audible, and tangible world was created. Outside this world there is nothing. Of course, there may be rays and vibrations as yet undiscovered, but that is something quite different. Sooner or later they will be discovered and will merely strengthen people's belief that everything is material. Ah, how you love fairy tales! And how we have to fight against them! In fact it is quite easy to understand how these tales arise. People do not want to die, the thought of death frightens them; they are frightened that they will never see the sun again—in fact, frightened of the word *never*. So they invent various consolations for themselves. Paramount in their minds is the desire that something should remain after death. But we do not deceive ourselves. We have no need. We do not depend on time, and we live as long as matter exists. And the kingdom of matter is eternal!"

The Devil sprang to his feet, jumped high in the air, somersaulted, and landed on the elephant's head in a blaze of purple flame, shouting:

"The kingdom of matter is eternal!"

Eternal, eternal . . . echoed the vaults of the inner halls, and the bats, rising in swarms, formed a strange black design above his head.

"Stop these acrobatics!" I said. "Maybe they impress some people, but *I* am much more interested in what you say. It seems that we have indeed been gravely mistaken about you."

The Devil jumped down and assumed the same pose as before, beside the feet of the elephant.

"You are mistaken from beginning to end," he said. "As much about us as about yourselves! Your first error, as I have already said, consists in taking us for creatures of another world. No other world exists, none whatsoever! At all events, we do not believe in it. Our nature actually dictates that we do not know and cannot know anything except the earth. I am astonished that you fail to understand this. But as I have already begun to speak plainly with you, I will tell you that the legend about the other world has, to a considerable extent, been created by us."

"I do not understand," said I.

"You see, people often indulge in strange fantasies. Among other things, these often prevent people from living and from occupying themselves with their own affairs. And so, to free them from these fantasies, or at least to render them harmless, we take one tactical, or to be more precise, pedagogical course of action. Namely, parallel with the harmful and distracting fantasies, we create others, resembling them, but harmless.

"Take those fantasies about the unreality of this world, the world beyond, everlasting life, eternity—in all that, there is something weakening, depriving people of the perseverance indispensable for life. You can see how the person who comes to believe in everlasting life begins to regard the present one with some contempt. He begins to place little value on the good things of life, is not so willing to fight for them, very often does not even wish to retrieve what is taken away from him. Just think what can come of such a situation. Generally he begins behaving strangely, spending too much time dreaming, experiencing mystical sensations, and finally resigning from life altogether.

"Mysticism—there's your chief evil. So we take pity on people, and, using some susceptible mind, we construct our own theory about the world beyond, life beyond the grave, everlasting life—call it what you will—a simple, consequential, logical theory, false though it may be. Nevertheless, you understand, I don't want to suggest that a genuine theory of a world beyond does exist—all are equally false. Undoubtedly there are theories of a certain unpleasant mystical or religious flavor; if these don't lead people straight into religious mania, they certainly corrupt them.

"Compared with these harmful fantasies, our theories are, between you and me, simply a small fabrication. There is nothing obscure, nothing mystical about them. We base everything on the most realistic earthly facts; it is just that they have never been, are not, and never can be true.

"As a result, our world beyond is not in any way different from the earth. It is merely, so to speak, the earth turned upside down. You realize that places with much in common, even seen upside down, are not dangerous.

"We are much helped in this situation by that basic error you make about us, and ultimately by the error you make about yourselves."

"And how, according to you, are we mistaken about ourselves?"

"I even find it hard to explain it to you," said the Devil, "your ideas are so confused. I must begin a long way back.

"In that old book of yours is written the story of Adam and Eve. Well now, that story is not correct, and this fallacious theory concerning the origin of man confuses all your subsequent ideas about him. As for the new theory of the origin of man from protoplasm, it is very witty. I admit that. But it is even further from the truth. I will now attempt to tell you what really happened.

"Adam and Eve are the names of those descended from the Great One. So they say; I do not know how true it is, but then I do not know that we can be sure of anything, probably not. But they do say that there was a Great One called the Bearer of Light, who fought and quarreled, not with heaven but with the earth, with matter, or with falsehood, and conquered it. It was not until much later, we said, that he quarreled with heaven.

"He rose very high, but they say that in the end he doubted the truth, and for a moment he believed in that very falsehood he had been fighting against. This caused him to fall and be smashed into a thousand pieces. And it is from his descendants that Adam and Eve came. With the best will in the world I cannot tell the story any better than that: you see, it borders on matters I don't understand. And what I don't understand does not exist. It is most unpleasant to speak about what is found on the edge of some emptiness beyond which nothing exists. We are afraid of this void. And there you have it: I have told you our biggest secret. It is on account of this fear, this terror, that we attach ourselves to you; you help us to ignore the dreadful nothingness and forget about it.

"But I will return to what I was talking about earlier. Adam and Eve, according to your old book, lived in paradise. This is the first error: they lived on earth. But, how can I put it? They only played at living on the earth—like children! And with nine-tenths of their being they lived in that emptiness we so detest and which is hostile to life. They called this void the world of the miraculous. To my way of thinking they were not normal, and they certainly suffered hallucinations of sight and hearing. Take the fact that they were reported to have seen God and spoken with Him. I don't know what that means, but it is undoubtedly something terrible."

I saw the Devil begin to tremble and huddle himself into his mantle.

"Of course, I do not believe in God. That would be ridiculous," he said. "But I pass on to you the legend as it stands. It is said that we rebelled against God: that is quite absurd. We never rebelled against God because we did not believe, do not believe, and can never believe in Him. The part of the legend dealing with our rebellion against God we invented ourselves. Later on I will tell you the reason.

"What is said about Adam and Eve further on in your book is again incorrect: it is written that they wanted to be like gods, and wanted to know what is good and what is evil. That is wrong, because they were like gods, and knew what is good and what is evil. To us this was most unpleasant and frightening."

The Devil became silent as if he found it difficult to speak.

"They were as if stronger than we," he continued. "Of course, all this was fantasy. But we were for them on the level of animals. They could see us only as animals. And they also gave us names, corresponding to our qualities."

The Devil pronounced the last words very unwillingly.

"I must also tell you," he continued, "that they were not alone on earth. The earth was inhabited by another race of people, the descendants of animals. But nothing is said in your book about this other race. They were completely in our power and could never get away from us. But we wanted, above all, to subordinate Adam and Eve. Their presence embarrassed us. We could not be sure of anything with them there. You see, they gave the impression that at any moment they could make the whole world disappear. They said that nothing existed and everything was merely a dream, and that it was possible to wake up and find everything gone."

The Devil lost his usual casual tone and seemed afraid to speak.

Looking at him at that moment, I realized that the basis of his nature was fear.

"These are words that are hard to utter," he said, looking at me like a beaten dog. "Still, now I have started, I had better continue.

"Thus the struggle started. The problem was to rid these two of their fantasies, to convince them that the world does exist; that life is not a game but a very serious, even difficult and troublesome thing, and that notions of good and evil are ultimately only relative and impermanent. To convince them would mean to banish them from paradise.

"This paradise really disgusted us. Perpetual talks about God, eternal love and kisses. We could not take it at all!"

"Why did it irritate you so?"

"Of course, you wouldn't understand. They said that love was their main strength and a powerful magic; that through love they would resurrect the Great One and thus restore the lost world. I don't understand it at all. But just think of it, how could we tolerate such a perverted philosophy? It was quite enough for us to accept the fact that they could vanish before our very eyes. You see, often a rose-colored cloud would come down and they vanished. We were powerless to prevent it, even though it disturbed us greatly. Besides, we found their costume positively dreadful—you know, the one Adam and Eve had before the Fall. We considered it highly improper. Matter demands a certain propriety. These two denied matter, and yet admired beauty."

The Devil drawled the word contemptuously.

"We tried to convince them that the body is essentially very ugly and indecent and much better covered up whenever possible. But they were not prepared to listen.

"It reached a point where their example began to have a bad effect on the other race, the descendants of the animals.

"'There remained only one way to get the better of

Adam and Eve: to introduce suffering into their life, and force them to believe in the reality of matter.

"But how? We thought for a long time. Finally, one of us turned our attention to the descendants of animals. The whole of their lives consisted of harboring grudges and endeavoring to get out of difficulties by burdening others with them. They had no doubts about the reality of this world, nor of material things. On the contrary, they were quite ready to smash each other's heads in for the tiniest thing—a pretty stone, for example. Their ideas of good and evil changed so quickly that even we could not keep up with them. In the morning the sun is good; at midday, evil; by evening, good again. In the evening, the wife is good; in the morning, evil; in the evening, good again; and so on.

"And we started wondering why everything went so well with them; perhaps it was something to do with their habits. It occurred to us that if only we could get Adam and Eve to take up one of these little ways, we might very well manage to convince them of the reality of things, and of the relativity of good and evil.

"Among the customs of the animal descendants was one which particularly entertained us—of all their ways this appeared to us to be the most idiotic. This was their habit of eating daily, and in great quantities, the fruit from a certain tree. They had a legend that in the distant past some god, who had come down to earth, had taught them to eat this fruit. They raised statues of this god and worshipped him. This was amusing enough, but still more comical was the fact that when they did not have this fruit, they actually suffered, and many even died. And so it was that those tribesmen who had a lot of fruit stored, or possessed many trees, were respected and considered wise and good, but those who had neither fruit nor trees were thought to be good-for-nothing and were sometimes even killed. We

came to the conclusion that if we could get Adam and Eve
to eat this fruit, we might succeed in making common sense
intelligible to them.

"So one of our number went to Eve and offered her one
of these fruits to taste. As I said, we could only appear before them in the shape of animals, so my colleague had to
take on the appearance of a snake.

"In your book it is written that they were forbidden to
eat the fruit of a certain tree. That is not true—nothing was
forbidden them. There was, however, much they did not
understand. They found great pleasure simply in looking at
this fruit of which the descendants of the animals ate so
greedily.

"When the snake brought Eve some of the fruit and
explained that it was edible, Eve ate it and gave some to
Adam. He too ate it, and they both began to enjoy this new
attraction. From that day on, the snake brought the fruit
regularly. They ate it in the morning, at midday, and in the
evening. Then the snake told them where to find the fruit
growing in abundance and taught them to gather it for
themselves. This new pastime they enjoyed also.

"I cannot tell you that they had never eaten before this.
But it is certain that earlier on, everything had been different: they had ascribed a special meaning to everything, and
they had felt magic in all things. Now, at last, there was
no magic at all in anything. They ate just as the descendants
of the animals did, for pleasure, or in order to pass the time.
And we watched them and waited to see where it would
lead.

"The results were not slow in coming.

"One day Eve noticed that she was putting on weight,
and this greatly distressed her. Then she began to see
strange things about Adam's conduct. Undeniably his love
was rapidly weakening. Once he yawned in the heat of

passionate kisses, a thing that had never happened before. Then he fell asleep when Eve was not ready for sleep and wanted him to tell her about the stars. After that Eve was sure that Adam's character was changing for the worse; she noticed it especially when he was hungry for the fruit; at such times he became irritable, nagging, and altogether insufferable. In the mornings, instead of his usual kisses and caresses, he had a passionate desire for the fruit, and until he had had his fill, he did not even glance at Eve. Eve was very offended by this, but even though she submitted unwillingly to the new routine she was at pains to prepare more of the fruit for Adam, so that he would be well fed and would not find fault with her.

"Observing it all, we were beside ourselves with delight. Adam and Eve began to take on a resemblance to ordinary people, that is, the descendants of the animals.

"Without being aware of it, Adam and Eve got into the habit of eating very much more fruit than was necessary. And in fact, they soon began to suffer when they had no fruit or when they thought the fruit was scarce. And whenever this happened they found it hard to talk about the unreality of things because the reality of the fruit spoke for itself. Otherwise, why should they not satisfy their needs with imaginary fruit? But imaginary fruit certainly did not satisfy them. They needed the real, genuine fruit of the earth in exactly the same way as the descendants of the animals.

"This was the beginning of our victory.

"A small cause sometimes has huge effects, and it was enough for Adam and Eve in the case of the fruit to admit the reality of matter for reality to seep into them from all directions.

"Adam and Eve soon realized that they lacked much that they needed. They would wish for things that were not

there and rage when they did not materialize. Discontentment with the world gradually took hold of them. Suffering
began increasingly to enter their lives. It was then that the
ridiculous, irrational joy they experienced on account of
trifles—a flower or a butterfly, sunshine, rain, wind, clouds,
thunderstorms, and goodness knows what besides—which
had disgusted us most, began to wane and in the end almost
completely disappeared. The sun, now, was burning them,
the rain drenched them, the thunderstorms frightened them,
the wind made them feel cold, and so on. At the same time,
the hallucinations they suffered came less often; what they
called the world of the miraculous gradually faded and vanished from their view. We were very glad, because although
it is certain that no such miraculous world exists, these
hallucinations frightened us. In general, everything that
they called magic ceased, and they lost the ability to disappear from us at will. However, even all this was only the
beginning. Things became serious from the time they
started to quarrel.

"You see, when this foolish magic business ceased, their
life became boring, though it was long before they became
aware of this. Discontentment with life and with their situation began, from time to time, to overflow into dissatisfac-
tion with one another. Misunderstandings arose, and finally
one fine day they had their first quarrel.

"This came about exactly as it usually does. Eve teased
Adam about the amount of fruit he had eaten that morning. More than likely, her joke did reveal certain hidden
resentments against Adam. Maybe it was not the first time
she had teased him like that. In any case it annoyed Adam,
for he felt the ache of hunger for the fruit in his stomach
and he was very disgruntled with himself. He answered Eve
sharply. Eve was offended and replied loudly that she could
not tolerate such a tone of voice, nor such treatment. They

began to argue, and within two minutes the quarrel was in full swing.

" 'You never listen to me properly, you always reply to the first half of a sentence,' Adam said, very nearly shouting. 'Let me speak . . .'

" 'You don't speak, you yell. I don't want to listen to you at all while you are in this mood,' said Eve, greatly irritated.

" 'Listen to me, you are interrupting me again, I say . . .'

" 'Yes, I'm interrupting you, and I will go on interrupting you, because I don't want to listen . . .'

"And so on in similar vein.

"They stood face to face and stared at each other with outright hatred. It was then that they first noticed they were naked. This seemed terribly wicked and shameful, especially to Eve. She ran off into the wood and made clothes for herself out of leaves. Adam, to show her that he was offended as well, made himself clothes too. They did not speak to each other for a whole day following this incident.

"After that, everything went as if rehearsed. They began to quarrel nearly every day, and soon they were arguing several times a day. No matter what Adam wanted, Eve unfailingly desired the opposite. She contradicted whatever he said, more often than not adding several very caustic remarks. They started disagreeing and ended up shouting and quarreling. Eve discovered a great many shortcomings in Adam. When he spoke to her, having entirely forgotten the previous day's quarrel, Eve, to him totally irrationally, would tell him exactly what she thought of him. At first, on such occasions, Adam would listen patiently without answering back. He simply sat and ate the fruit which Eve, in spite of everything, still prepared for him. Later on, however, some really uncalled-for remark would provoke him, and he would start to object. Eve would take offense at his retort; Adam would raise his voice. They would begin to speak at the same time and interrupt each other, and so the quarrel proceeded. Every day there was some new development, so that it was impossible to tell what they were going to quarrel about next.

"There was no harmony in their lives any more. If Eve wanted to go out somewhere for a visit, Adam had to gather fruit. If Eve wanted Adam to stay at home, he always found somewhere he had to go. Then Eve would feel hurt that he had left her alone, and of course, she immediately convinced herself that Adam had gone to Lilith, his first wife, whom he had divorced when God created Eve.

"Well, it all ended like this: after one of the worst rows, Eve left the cave where she lived with Adam, vowing never to return. The next day she sent her maid for her things."

"Maid?" I asked.

"Well, yes, maid," said the Devil. "Adam was terribly angry, then frightened. He asked for forgiveness and swore he would never hurt Eve again. But Eve did not return. And it seemed to Adam that the monkeys who lived in the palm trees in front of the cave were all laughing at him and shouting: 'Here is Adam, abandoned by Eve!'

"A long time later they were reconciled. But you must understand that things were not the same now. There was no longer any magic in their lives. Eve blamed Adam for this. Adam thought the fault lay with Eve. For this reason they started quarreling again, Eve went away again, and so on. In the end Adam got himself at one fell swoop three more wives from a dark tribe living nearby, and Eve took up with a young faun who played the flute of a morning. The faun turned out to be very stupid and soon bored her, so she made friends with a nymph from a mountain stream and declared all men to be completely uninteresting.

"After this they were ours. Adam began to earn his own bread by the sweat of his brow, but whenever possible, he would follow the example of the descendants of the animals, preferring not to earn his bread, but to take it from others or to make them work for him.

"The legend about paradise, however, persisted among the descendants of Adam and Eve for a long time, and it was reputed that their ancestors were exiled from paradise because of some crime. This is actually our version of the story, and we made several more changes at the same time. For instance, we let people think that it is we who are the descendants of the Great One, and that the Great One rebelled against God. We twisted the facts so thoroughly that only a few people are capable of unraveling the truth. That is why, as I told you at the beginning of our talk, it is so difficult for me to explain the real position to you. You see, you are in error quite as much on our account as on your own.

"The descendants of Adam interbred with the descendants of the animals to such a degree that it became quite difficult to distinguish them. As a result, there came about many curious situations and misunderstandings. At times even we could not tell the difference between them. For instance, many of us would buy souls of the descendants of Adam, only to find that they had no souls. This happened because the descendants of the animals pretended to be the descendants of Adam, and even we fell for it."

"So the descendants of the animals have no souls?"

"Of course not. Souls do not exist as such. What is a soul? It is only a collective term for the diverse phenomena of psycho-physical life. On the other hand, the existence of some kind of soul is admitted by the descendants of Adam, that is, the genuine descendants of Adam. They think of it as something like a family heirloom which is handed down by successive generations. Sometimes we buy these souls when they are for sale. You see, we are collectors and we collect things which have neither value nor meaning to anybody except us."

The Devil was obviously rather confused.

"The thing is that this interbreeding with the animals' descendants," he continued, "is only external. Our tradition maintains that so long as the descendants of Adam retain their souls they can go away from us."

"Does that frighten you?"

"Oh, yes. But we love them! So we make every effort to prevent them from going away."

"How do you do it then?"

"Ah well, we use many different methods. First of all, of course, we endeavor to prevent their separation from the descendants of the animals. That is our main problem.

"Without realizing it, the descendants of Adam are trying the whole time to separate themselves from the descendants of the animals. We struggle against this separation, either by assuring Adam's descendants that the descendants of animals are their brothers, and have souls like their own, or on the contrary, by convincing them that they are all descendants of the animals and that none of them has a soul. You grasp our idea, the idea of equality and fraternity. More than anything else, it discourages the separation of the two. But the descendants of Adam are unable to carry such a load for long, and they are constantly sinking under the weight of it and surrendering to those same descendants of animals. As a result the descendants of animals have taken possession of the earth and the descendants of Adam are serving them."

"But why do they serve? I still don't understand," I said.

"Because the descendants of the animals are unable to manage without the descendants of Adam," said the Devil.

"You see, they cannot do anything on their own; like monkeys, all they can do is copy what the descendants of Adam have done, or alternatively destroy whatever comes their way. But Adam's descendants can create and destroy endlessly. Where they lead, all life follows. Without them the descendants of the animals would not have got far. But Adam's descendants are not free, they are subordinate to the animals. That is why they so often destroy what they themselves have built."

"Are the descendants of the animals not even capable of destruction then?"

"Oh, they destroy all right," said the Devil. "They can destroy very well. In fact they can even build too, only . . . how shall I put it . . . after a pattern that already exists. The point is that in general everything they do by themselves, even destruction, is talentless and marked by utter futility, a combination of boredom, apathy, and absurdity. I expect you have seen this kind of work. It is for this reason that the descendants of Adam are generally valued, although it is essential to keep them firmly in hand. But the descendants of the animals are not as helpless as they used to be in the early days.

"They have evolved markedly during that time, that is, since the death of Adam. Take a look at the whole of contemporary culture, techniques of engineering, industry, and commerce.

"During the same period Adam's descendants have remained virtually on the same level as before. You understand, for descendants of Adam, evolution does not exist. They have everything, only they do not know it, and they consider themselves to be something quite different from what they are. Yet when they come across something that they have in fact forgotten about, that very thing they regard in the light of evolution. But this deception, which applies to everything they encounter, lies entirely in their own minds.

"To continue, the descendants of Adam have a great many prejudices, and a kind of atavism which prevents them from living for the present. The descendants of animals do not have any trace of this atavism. For instance, basically the descendants of Adam place no value on things and attach little significance to material wealth. They don't have sufficient flexibility of mind and of imagination— qualities which are, on the other hand, very highly developed among the descendants of the animals."

"Flexibility?"

"Well, yes. The descendants of Adam only vaguely understand, for instance, that it is possible to think of one thing, say another, and do a third. Their intellect is not capable of grasping such ideas, or seeing that a person can have completely different standards for himself and for others, whereby he can, for instance, allow and condone any act he performs himself, while forbidding and condemning the same thing in another. Essentially they wish everything to be constant, that a truth proved in one case should be equally true in all other cases. But the descendants of the animals rightly think that would make life very dull. There would be no variety.

"All this shows, of course, a certain narrow-mindedness in the descendants of Adam. I should add, furthermore, while we are on the subject, that they are never satisfied with form and appearances, but are always striving for the essence, thereby creating for themselves many unnecessary problems. Take, for example, religious questions. The descendants of the animals happen also to be very religious, but their religion does not interfere with their lives. They are able to adapt it to suit their way of life. If they do something particularly unpleasing, they usually say they are acting out of religious motives, and that it is the will of God.

"When the descendants of animals pray, they always ask God to give them something, mainly things belonging to their neighbors which they covet. If they meet a person who does not pray as they do but in quite a different manner, they think it not unworthy of praise to give him a kick in the teeth. This tendency has had many interesting consequences and has contributed much to the livening-up of history. Adam's descendants do not understand any of this. They do not know how to separate religion from life and draw, as it were, two parallel lines.

"The descendants of animals understand perfectly that life is a raw deal and that sentiment has no place in it. They understand that in life, might is right, and they act accordingly. The descendants of animals always imagine that somebody wants to take away from them what they consider to be their property. Nine-tenths of their time, or sometimes all ten-tenths, is occupied with thoughts of how to keep intact what belongs to them, and how to acquire the belongings of their fellow men.

"Adam's descendants always give way to them in this respect as in many others. And, besides, many of them adhere to the fantasies of old, for you see they still retain dim memories of life before the Fall."

"You still consider these fantasies to be a danger then?"

"They are not dangerous," said the Devil, "but all the same we think it advisable to be forewarned and take precautions."

"But what precautions can you take? I don't understand."

"There are various ways," said the Devil. "I will tell you about two particularly amusing cases."

.　.　.

"There was once a hermit who studied various ways of interpreting the world, religious teachings, doctrines both secret and well known, and such writings as were available at that time. Among these he found a number of misrepresentations, deliberate as well as unintentional. He expounded his investigations in a tome which he intended to have printed.

"I came to him in the guise of a hermit, and said:

" 'You are writing a book?'

" 'Yes,' he said.

" 'You want to tell people the truth, the whole truth without any concealment as you understand it?'

" 'Yes,' he said. 'I believe that to be the best way. The truth has been hidden from the people for far too long.'

" 'I see your point,' said I. 'I endorse your opinion, sympathize with your point of view, and find it exceptionally noble and valuable. For all that, I should not print your book.'

" 'Why?' he asked, at a loss.

" 'Because, my kind and dear friend, you still do not understand the emotion which has been your guiding principle.'

" 'What kind of emotion would that be?' he asked.

" 'What kind? I will tell you. It is egoism! Egoism and striving for self-assertion, selfishness!'

"He was staggered.

" 'Egoism,' he said. 'But I never considered myself.'

" 'You did not consider yourself,' I said sarcastically, 'and whom did you think you were considering? Was it others that you were thinking of, then? Did you give thought to the fact that your book will destroy their beliefs, will deprive them of hope and consolation? No, you have not thought about that! But, according to you, that is not egoism. No, my esteemed friend, it is a common native intelligence speaking in you. You wanted to show people your truth. Where is your love of others in that? Where the moral? Where the sense of duty? Where the striving to help people, to alleviate the burdens of their life? You have found your truth for yourself; keep it to yourself, then. Do not rob people of their truth. Light your own fire, do not put out someone else's.' And so forth, and so on.

"Would you believe it, this nonsense impressed him deeply.

" 'What should I do?' he asked.

" 'Do not think only of yourself,' I said.

"And I gave him plenty of useful advice. As a result the work of the hermit became a collection of lies; his book was later quoted as proof of those very theories he wanted to disprove."

"The other case was even more amusing.

"A large crowd of people once joined together and decided to fight against evil. It was a very naive suggestion, for people have been fighting evil from the beginning of time. As a result of this opposition, evil is growing and flourishing. So at first we paid no attention to them. But later on, matters proved worse than we had thought. A dangerous idea had occurred to these people. 'There is no need for active opposition,' they said. 'Active resistance strengthens evil. We will do our utmost only to make people understand what is good and what is evil. Let us explain to them in every single case where evil is, of what the evil consists, and whence it springs!' You can imagine how this explanation of evil began to have results soon felt by all of us. Our fraternity became uneasy. I was entrusted with dealing with the problem.

"I put two plans into operation.

"First of all, I assembled the descendants of the animals. I tried to bring home to them the potential danger to society represented by the activity of these people who sought to fight against evil. I spoke many fine words on culture, civilization, the common good, the necessity for sacrifice, and so on. As a result, the struggle with evil was declared to be a crime which weakened and corrupted mankind.

"Afterwards, I went to the people who were struggling against evil and made an effort to win their confidence. Eventually, choosing an appropriate moment, I asked them: 'Whom do you serve?' They were embarrassed. 'You see, you yourselves do not know,' I said. 'You say that you are fighting evil. But can you possibly believe that evil would exist on earth unless God allowed it? As evil does exist on earth, obviously it must be part of the plan of the Higher Being. Can you really believe that the Higher Being could not cope with evil if He had to? You do not seem to understand that evil is a means of perfecting mankind. Suffering is very often the only way that one can come to understand higher spiritual truths. And you want to struggle against it! Can't you understand that you are fighting against the plan of the Higher Being, against the evolution of mankind? Besides, all evil is relative. Something that is evil at one level of evolution can be good at an earlier stage because it provides the essential stimulus for development. But you want to judge everything by your own standards. You have reached a comparatively high level and so you see what you fight against as evil. Just think of the others, those who are at an earlier stage of development. Do not bar them from the path toward progress and evolution!'

"If only you could have seen the effect it had on them! Deep in thought, they dispersed. And soon every one of them had written a book in which each in his own way proved the inevitability and necessity of evil.

"These books were a great success. Gradually the

struggle against evil turned into the justification of evil. Even the authors did not notice what was happening. It was exceptionally easy to do, because the justification of evil was by then far from being a crime; it was, on the contrary, considered to be honorable and deserving of every encouragement. Eventually it reached a point where there was literally no evil which those who had been fighting evil were not prepared to justify.

"These two cases were among the more difficult ones. I found it much easier to cope with the others. Sometimes when I noticed the appearance of unhealthy fantasies, I told people that they were a secret which had to be kept from the uninitiated. This has a wonderful effect on people. First, they begin to pride themselves on being initiated, and secondly, they begin to discover new 'secrets,' just the ones I need.

"Love of neighbors and secrets, these are my favorite weapons. Scattering the seeds of falsehood in these areas yields particularly rich harvests. This is especially useful in the battle against mysticism. Mysticism is the most dangerous thing for the descendants of Adam to get hold of. It is on the basis of a shared mysticism that they can recognize one another. There is an old prophecy that Adam's descendants will unite on a 'mystical quest,' conquer the descendants of the animals, and rule the world."

"Could that ever happen?"

"I should think not," said the Devil contemptuously. "In any case, we are always on the alert to prevent such things from happening.

"And there is also the fact that Adam's descendants all have a deeply held belief, however foolish, that all their everyday life is sleep, and they long to wake up and see something quite different."

"And you are afraid that they will wake up?" I said.

"Of course the possibility exists," said the Devil. "Which is where I began. I've already told you how much work and self-sacrifice is demanded of us just to keep you on earth."

"I cannot see any self-sacrifice," I said.

"No, you can't see it. Of course you can't see it because I have not shown you anything yet. Those examples I cited refer to people susceptible to lies. But we do have some very difficult cases indeed. In fact, to tell you the truth, the most reliable solution is the very one we used for Adam. Only now this method demands much more work and self-sacrifice. It was easy enough for the serpent to bring Eve the fruit. Now we need quite different guises. Many of us have to give up our lives in order to keep some obstinate person on earth.

"And that is not all. Our main danger is that from time to time the descendants of Adam realize how numerous they are and they begin to find ways of drawing closer to each other. That is the danger.

"As long as they live separately, we can cope with them in the same way as we did with Adam. But when they join together, when hotbeds of infection spring up all over the place, and when those breeding grounds begin to spread and connect up, it is then that we feel the danger, and we have to resort to other, more powerful means.

"I would like to show you a remarkable instance of self-sacrifice on our part. You people are not capable of anything like it."

The Devil stretched out his hand. The rock wall to the right of me parted, and became bathed in evening sunlight. I saw a street in Colombo, near Victoria Park. On all sides were gardens with low trellises or stone walls. It was only here and there that the distant roofs and verandahs of houses could be seen. Flowering trees; the "fire tree" with bright-red, flat-capped flowers; trees of many colors—light-blue, yellow, or mauve; the pink earth, peculiar to Ceylon; crossroads marked by huge banyan trees, mammoth in comparison with the other trees; and the thick, yellow bamboos with dark leaves. This part of Colombo is truly a garden city.

In the middle of the street a black rickshaw bowled along. In the carriage sat a man in a white suit and a wide-brimmed sun helmet of the kind usually worn in Ceylon. I recognized in him an acquaintance of mine, a young Englishman called Leslie White.

I had met him a few months before in the south of Ceylon, at a feast in a Buddhist monastery. Afterwards we sat together for a long time in the cell of a learned *bhikku,* discussing Buddhism. Leslie White was, in many respects, unlike the usual middle-class colonial Englishman. He was completely lacking in the absurd snobbery of the Civil Service; he pursued his many interests with zeal and sincerity; he never tried to affect that tone of mocking indifference to everything in the world but sport—sport is the one thing supposed to be taken seriously; and he did not hide his liking for the natives. This demanded great independence in a country where a minor bank clerk is ashamed to be seen talking to a Brahmin in public.

He had lived in Ceylon for two years, and held a post under the Governor. He studied the local languages, and, risking his personal reputation as well as his position in the Service, he had many friends among the Singhalese and Tamils. He treated local English society very coolly and was seldom to be seen in it. He read a great deal, studied Indian religions and Indian art; he understood many things about the East of which we have much to learn, and gave thought to the significance Eastern ideas could have for the West. We often met and discussed such matters. I enjoyed his company, for although so knowledgeable, he was not in the least pedantic. He liked horses and the sea and owned a catamaran, a narrow boat resembling a spider, which he took out to sea with the native fishermen, occasionally disappearing for several days at a time.

For him, work was no more than an inevitable evil. He had already been marked down as a person who would not go far in the Service and who would have been better placed in an academic post. Altogether, he contrasted sharply with the heroes of Kipling and seemed to me to represent a new type of Englishman in India, born after Kipling and still very rare.

The rickshaw stopped by a garden trellis beyond which a two-story bungalow was just visible. Now I knew whom Leslie was visiting. An Indian-Tamil lived there; he was wealthy and well known in Ceylon, and I had met him several months before, shortly before I left. I remembered I had written to Leslie about him.

This Indian was already an old man, and cultivated in the European sense. He told me many very interesting things about Yogis and Yoga. Talking to him, I always felt that he knew much more than he was saying. I met him under rather peculiar circumstances and at our first meeting I completely failed to understand him. But soon I was convinced that he was the only person who could help me discover the real, miraculous India.

I greatly wanted Leslie to meet him and talk to him. They had met previously, but only on official occasions. Now I gathered that Leslie had followed my advice and come to see him at home.

The rickshaw boy trotted away from the garden gates, and Leslie walked between the flower beds up to the house with the big verandah. He was met first by two white-turbaned servants and then ushered in by his host, who was dressed in a European tussore frock coat.

After a few minutes they sat down and began to talk.

"Yoga and everything that is connected with it has interested me for a long time. I have read everything I could get hold of on the subject," Leslie was saying. "It seems to me that Yoga can answer many of our questions. I would dearly like to see the practical results of Yoga so as to convince myself that it is more than just theories.

"I understand the basic idea. To practice Yoga, each individual must live his whole life according to what he has decided to do with it: the musician, the merchant, the soldier, each must live, eat, and breathe differently. This will cause his work to be of the highest standard, and as such will be for him a means of spiritual purification. It strikes a European as preposterous that if I want to study philosophy, I must eat in a special way. But I understand this. The way I see it, the supreme aim of Yoga is to eradicate discord and close the abyss between the ideological and the practical side of life by way of making everything material subordinate to ideas. I understand all this in theory. However, I want to know whether in fact Yoga does give the miraculous results claimed for it."

"You understand the basic essence of Yoga completely," the Indian replied. "Yoga is precisely the harnessing of life in the yoke of ideas. You know that the word 'Yoga' has the same root as your word 'yoke'."

"Yes," Leslie replied. "I know that. And I find it interesting and of paramount importance that the East understands the need to unite all the trivial things of life with the highest ideological aspirations in such a way that nothing would remain isolated, or superfluous. I understand that to a Yogi every step and every breath is a prayer which draws him ever nearer to the ideal. And here we find the main difference between the East and the West. We build our ideal separately from life, and life separately from the ideal. We accept petty, insignificant, vulgar, and often disgusting and brutal reality, but we console ourselves with the beauty of our ideals.

"You want every minute of your life to be imbued with the ideal and to serve it. I understand all this, but tell me, are there ever any real results achieved by Yoga, or does it all come down to travelers' tales of India? Do you understand, I want to know whether all these miraculous happenings I have read about in books on Yoga ever really took place—clairvoyance, second sight, mind-reading, thought-transference, knowledge of the future, and the like. I often wake up at night [I suddenly felt that Leslie was speaking from the depths of his soul] and think, can it really be true that somewhere there are people who have achieved something miraculous? I know I would drop everything to follow such a person. But I must be sure that he has succeeded. You must understand me. I cannot believe in words any longer. Too often have we been deceived by words, and I cannot deceive myself any more, nor do I want to. Tell me then, are there people who have attained something and what is it they have attained, and could I attain the same and how?"

Leslie fell silent, and I saw that the old Indian looked at him with a quiet and affectionate smile as if he were a child.

"Yes, there are such people," he said slowly. "And you can see them. If you come to me and tell me that this is what you want, you will see them. Only you must realize that this cannot happen all at once, in one day. If you really want to learn, I will tell you: Friend, come and live with me, try to understand our thoughts, try to learn to think in a new way. To learn from a teacher, it is necessary to understand him. That demands long preparation. Meanwhile I will inquire about the whereabouts of a teacher of my acquaintance. We do not use the post or the telegraph. In two weeks' time, a man is going to travel to India, to Puri. There in the temple, he will ask where the teacher can be found, and perhaps he will find someone who knows and through whom he can let the teacher know that we would like to see him. Then in the same way, through somebody else, the teacher will let us know when he will be coming here or where we should go to meet him. Sometimes he lives in the country, near a small village in the jungle, or in the mountains; sometimes you can find him in one of the big temples in Madras or Tandur, or somewhere else. But it is necessary to wait patiently. The pupil must stand at the door and wait until the teacher calls him. It could be tomorrow, it could be in a month's time, or it could be in a year."

I saw that Leslie was listening intently, but also that he was not at all happy with what the Indian was saying.

"And the teacher you are speaking of, has he attained those things I have read about in books?"

The Indian smiled again.

"What is it, according to you, he should attain? You yourself admit and agree that the aim of Yoga is the subjection of life to an ideal. Isn't that an attainment in itself, if each minute of a person's life is subject to the search for higher meaning? Is it not an attainment that the person is free of those inner contradictions of which your whole life is composed? Is it not attainment to have that inner peace, silence, and calm, which reigns in the soul of a teacher? And since you speak of supernatural psychic forces, a teacher does possess them, although he does not attach any significance to them. It may be that he will see fit to show you his powers. But you cannot demand that he should, you cannot make it a condition. The teacher himself decides what you need. And you must trust him."

I could see that there was a great conflict in Leslie's soul. He felt drawn toward his companion and he liked him. He wanted to believe him, but at the same time his European mind could not agree with what the Indian was saying and how he was saying it.

"You say that you are prepared to leave everything," continued the old man. "But that is not necessary at all. On the contrary, it is very often more important to continue one's life as before and to subject this life to your higher endeavor. Look at me. You know me. I occupy myself with politics and business, and live as a family man. I have not left anything. To retreat into a wilderness is often the easiest way, but you must not always do what is easiest. Sometimes it is necessary to take the more difficult path. Later on, the teacher will tell you what you need to do. I can tell you only one thing—learn to think in a new way. For as long as you are ignorant of the right way of thinking, it will always seem to you that what I am saying leaves out something important."

"I would just like to see the actuality," said Leslie. "When I have seen that, I will be easy in my mind in regard to the rest, and I will do everything I am told. You do see my point, my intellectual conscience does not allow me to accept the existence of objective facts on faith. To acknowledge them as facts, I must see them."

The old Indian smiled again.

"If you will follow the way of Yoga," he said, "a whole series of changes will begin to take place in your soul. First of all, you will start to discover a succession of new and different values. And along with the appearance of these new values, the old ones will begin to pale and disappear.

And then, perhaps, that which at present you hold to be most important will seem quite unimportant. This cannot be explained in words, it can only be felt. Only one who has lived through such inner upheavals will understand me. In fact, everyone has had some experience of this in the passage from childhood to adulthood. To children, toys, games, school activity, the opinion of teachers, all seem incredibly important. Then think how insignificant all that seems to a youth who loses his heart to a woman. At such moments he shuns his comrades, for their conversations sound ridiculous to him. In the same way, in the soul of a Yogi a new love blossoms, and all the values of ordinary life he sees as children's toys. So it will be with the facts you seek, for they may not seem so important to you eventually."

"That may be," said Leslie. "But why then do they constantly speak about these facts, why refer to them and build everything on them? One cannot refer to facts which have not been proved."

"If you speak like that, you do not understand," said the Indian. "He who understands speaks of other matters, the inner, not the outer life. At the beginning, you were on the right track. It is necessary to eradicate the conflict between the life of ideas and the life of everyday. In order to achieve this, it is necessary that you should know yourself. Each moment, know what you are doing and why. Only then will you be the master of things rather than their slave. Usually you carry out your wishes before you have given any thought as to whether or not they are necessary for your higher aims. Try to live in such a way that you keep a watch on your actions and do nothing that does not serve the higher purpose. Or, to put it another way, learn to do everything in such a way that whatever you do serves a higher purpose. It is possible to do that. If something is particularly difficult, look upon it as an exercise. Remember, everything which you do that is difficult, you do in order to subject yourself to the spirit. Then everything will become easier and everything will have meaning. But whatever you are doing, it is vital that you ask yourself, before each thought, before each word, before each action: Why am I doing this? Is this necessary? Then, imperceptibly, a number of your actions and deeds will cease to be unnecessary and they will start to serve the higher aims. The inner conflict in your life will begin to disappear and be replaced by harmony. Then learn to give yourself rest; this, possibly, is the most important. Learn not to think, learn to control your thoughts. Ask yourself frequently whether it is necessary to think about what you are thinking, or might it be better to think about something else, or better still, not to think at all? This is the most difficult of all, but it is essential. Learn to think and not to think, at will. Know how to stop thoughts. Be able to create inner silence within yourself. The moment will come when you will hear the voice of silence. This is the first and most important Yoga. When this comes, when you begin to hear the voice of silence and stillness, then those new forces and abilities you talk of can begin to appear in you. At first they will be vague and imprecise, but later they will become as obedient to your will as sight, hearing, and touch. But everything should be accepted calmly, without hurry; without forced attention to inner progress—attention can prevent the growth of new capacities. Then it is necessary to learn to see every object as a whole. Do you understand what this means? Normally you see only the parts of a thing, either only the beginning, without any continuation, and the end; or the middle, or the end. Always set yourself to see everything as a whole. To reach this viewpoint, start to think of everything in reverse; do not take the beginning without the end. And then you will begin to see much more in things than you see at present. What is clairvoyance? We are now sitting on the verandah and we see a part of the garden. If you wish to see the whole garden, you must go up to the next floor. If you go higher still, you will see the whole town. A clairvoyant is a person who can see more than others. To see more, you must climb higher. That is the whole secret."

"But what does it mean, climbing higher?" said Leslie. "I see that at some times it may be possible, at other times impossible; but in what sense is 'climbing' used? In the sense of abstract meditation on objects or on other kinds of things? And what will the result be? Will it lead one to any kind of new powers? And once again the same question: is there someone who possesses these powers? I cannot believe that I would be the first!"

"You will not be the first," said the Indian. "However, in order eventually to achieve this, you must first of all realize how far from it you are at this moment. You are like a child who is crying because his father does not permit him to mount his spirited warhorse, does not put his own gun into his hand, nor his heavy sharp saber. The child must first grow up, then he will receive everything. And in any case, at present he could not have made use of anything. He could lift neither gun nor sword, and the horse would throw him immediately. First become master of what you have, and afterwards try for greater things. Analyze your day. Is much of your time given up to a search for higher things? Try to ask yourself every hour what you have done during that hour. Yogis ask themselves every minute. Continual practice is necessary to gain self-control. At present the whole of your life consists of compromise in one way or another. How do you expect to develop your power of endurance?

"You probably go in for sports?"

Leslie nodded his head.

"What is your favorite sport—football, cricket?"

"Polo," said Leslie.

"Very well then, polo. Surely you understand the necessity of training for polo. It is equally necessary to train both yourself and your pony. Both of you need daily exercise. Imagine that for three months you did not mount the pony and you have spent your nights in a club playing cards. Your pony is left standing in the stables for three months and the lazy groom does not even bother to exercise him every day. And imagine taking part in a big match. How will it turn out? Have you any chance of winning? You know very well there is not the slightest hope. You will have neither the strength nor the dexterity nor the endurance. Your pony will not obey you. He will tire at the very beginning of the game, and you will tire even earlier. Since you know from past experience that this is true of polo, why will you not admit the same about your soul? It has to become accustomed gradually to the new order of ideas, to the new plan of life. And when you begin to achieve something, then, together with the blossoming of new powers in your soul, you will begin to notice that you are no longer alone on the path. Though all around the night will be dark, everywhere on the path you will begin to see lights, and you will understand that these are travelers who are going in the same direction with you, to the same temple, to the same feast."

Leslie sat and listened, and I could see that, in spite of the abundance of Eastern metaphors, usually unpalatable to a European, the main content of what the Indian was saying corresponded very much to what he had himself been thinking. Nearly all of what he heard, Leslie had read or had heard of previously. Nevertheless, his companion impressed him as a person who knew. With the cool good sense of an Englishman, Leslie got the gist of what the old Indian was saying. And I saw that in Leslie's heart, along with sympathy and spontaneous gratitude to the old man, a firm and definite decision was developing.

"What must I do to follow the way?" he said. "So far I find nothing to daunt me."

"Begin to observe yourself," said the Indian. "Try to limit yourself, even if it is only a matter of cutting out what you do not need anyway, but which takes most of your time and energy. Try to understand that you are a long way from the beginning of the way. And soon, in the distance, you will see the way."

The pictures were changing before my eyes. Leslie was again traveling in a rickshaw, and I saw that he was repeating the words of the Indian to himself and trying to sort them out. He had raised objections during his talk with the old man, but in reality everything he heard had made a much bigger impression on him than he had shown.

This interested me very much. Leslie was a persistent person. I felt that if he took something on, he would not compromise. It occurred to me that if anything could be achieved by way of Yoga, then he would achieve it. He had a great sense of adventure and the courage of a pioneer, always blazing new trails. He had a spark which did not allow him to be content with a peaceful life in a civilized place. He was the kind of man who discovers new countries.

The rickshaw was rolling through dark gardens. Leslie was sitting in the carriage, holding his topi on his knee. Strange to say, he was not alone. Along the left side of the rickshaw, some small creature was running. Looking intently I saw that this was a little devil. He was small, with a potbelly on disproportionately thin legs, and his fairly good-natured features were of a Chinese cast. The only oddity in his face was the narrow, unsympathetic lips, which he constantly licked with his long, thin tongue. He had small horns on the forehead and in his yellow eyes, small and shrewd, shone cunning and some secret thought. He ran very quickly, with tiny mincing steps, but without any effort, as if it did not matter to him. With a naughty smile he grabbed sometimes at the thin shaft of the carriage, apparently attempting to hamper the black rickshaw runner. At least twice he entangled himself in his legs, so that the rickshaw boy stumbled and nearly fell. And when Leslie arrived at the station, I noticed that the runner was soaked in sweat and breathing hard, as if he had been running in the heat.

"You see," the Devil told me, "this one has been appointed to look after him in order to prevent him from committing too many follies."

"Where did he come from?" I asked. "How and what can he prevent?"

"How he will prevent it is his business," said the Devil. "What he must prevent, you can guess for yourself. We consider Yoga to be playing with fire. He who is carried away by it loses connection with earth. The danger is much greater than you think. These silly ideas spread, and sometimes we have to resort to extreme measures. Take this Leslie White. You are right. If he takes up something, he will not let go. That is where the danger lies. That is why this little devil is attached to him. This is a very clever and good little devil. He genuinely and sincerely loves people. Even I do not quite understand him. But at the same time I agree that in this particular case he will achieve more than, say, I would. Sometimes one can only influence by kindness. But see what is happening now."

The train arrived. Leslie entered the first-class compartment, and the train rolled further on along the seashore. I knew this place well. Leslie was traveling out of town to the hotel where he was staying. This hotel stands on the seashore, on a rocky promontory, surrounded on three sides by water. Along both sides of the hotel, to the north toward Colombo and to the south, stretch sandy beaches dotted with coconut palms and small fishing villages.

Leslie arrived at the hotel and went directly to his room facing the sea, to dress for dinner. The black servant had already put out his soft shirt, collar, and dinner jacket. But when Leslie looked at his clothes, he anticipated the tedium of the same people, the same conversations.

"Why must I have dinner?" he asked himself. "Am I hungry, or have I only so little strength?"

It made him laugh.

"The old man was right," he continued to think. "What an incredible amount of time we waste on things that are quite unnecessary. If one could observe oneself, even for a little while, how much more time and strength one could save, instead of allowing it all to be dissipated on one unnecessary thing after another."

There were books lying on the table which he had received only that morning. Leslie knew from experience that after dinner he would want to go to sleep. But now he wanted to read, to think.

He rang the bell.

"I am not having dinner," he said to the boy who appeared noiselessly. "Bring me a small whisky and a large soda, two lemons, and some more ice."

Then, feeling immense relief, Leslie washed and put on his pajamas.

The boy brought a bottle of soda water, ice in a glass, two tiny green Ceylon lemons the size of walnuts, and a little whisky at the bottom of a tall glass. He set it all out on the table and silently put a square of paper and a pencil in front of Leslie. This was the usual ritual. Leslie had to write a chit for the buffet.

Leslie squeezed the two lemons into the glass, added ice, and a dash of whisky, poured some water, took a sip, lit his short, blackened pipe and sat down at the table in a comfortable wicker armchair, armed with one of his new books and a paper knife. He cut the book. But in his mind, as far as I could see, the talk with the Indian still continued.

Suddenly I noticed the little devil again. He had a very embarrassed and puzzled expression. He walked around the room, waddling ridiculously on his short, spindly legs, licking his narrow protruding lips, obviously looking for Leslie. It was a most weird spectacle. The little devil had lost Leslie and could not find him. Again and again he came up to the table where Leslie sat. He was like someone hypnotized, who has been told he will not be able to see his close friend. So there he was, fumbling about, even touching Leslie's knee, but bewildered, walking on. He clearly sensed that all was not well with him, but could not understand what was wrong.

Yes, indeed what I saw was certainly a very curious phenomenon. This more than anything else revealed to me the real relation of devil to man, a devil's true nature, and his fear of losing a man. Evidently, though my devil did not tell me this, it happened much more often than they wished.

At first I thought that the disappearance of Leslie depended on the book he was reading, and I looked over his shoulder. I knew this book, even knew the author, whose views I had always found rather too narrow. However, when I took a look at Leslie, I understood that the clue lay not in the book, but in the way he was reading it. His whole being was immersed in the world of ideas, material reality did not exist for him.

So that is the secret, I thought. To get away from reality means to get away from the devil, to become invisible to

him. This is excellent, for it signifies, conversely, that people
of dull reality, practical, workaday people, in general all
ordinary sober people, belong absolutely and completely to
the devil. To be frank, I was delighted by this discovery.

The poor little devil, apparently despairing of finding
Leslie, went and sat in the corner by the door, tucking his
legs under him. Watching him intently, I saw that he was
crying, wiping the tears away with his small fist, and altogether looking very miserable. Studying him, I realized
that he was really suffering and that his suffering was not
purely egoistic. He was actually afraid for Leslie, who had
suddenly disappeared to some place he could not imagine.
It was as if some silly woman had fallen for Leslie, and was
incapable of understanding his thoughts and interests; she
would suffer like this, and there would be times when she
too would be unable to find him, when she would sit in a
corner and whimper.

For some unknown reason very vivid pictures of such a
relationship came into my mind. The Leslie I knew was
young, full of life, hope, and prospects. And the woman
was plain, unintelligent, and dull. Both socially and intellectually she was infinitely inferior to Leslie. Leslie can
never allow himself to be seen with her nor introduce her
to anybody, nor even tell anybody about her. Probably she
is Eurasian, and she undoubtedly has some dubious past; it
is possible that she belongs, in the words of Kipling, to the
"oldest profession." Where Leslie found her, how he got
mixed up with her, and why he cannot leave her, is his
secret. There is certainly something very unpleasant about
it. He must hide her. It will be the end of career and prospects for Leslie White if her existence becomes known. He
will not be received anywhere, he will have to leave the
Service and go away; at one stroke he will be a ruined
man. The woman knows this, and yet with all her strength

she tries to keep her hold on him. And she succeeds, except for those moments when Leslie slips away from her. Why? What does Leslie keep her for? What is her hold on him? Why doesn't a man as strong and clever as Leslie cast this trash out of his life? It is quite incomprehensible. Probably there is something in her that he needs. Probably she appeals to some dark force in him. Such women can only keep their hold on men by appealing to their baser instincts.

My own thoughts astonished me. How had I guessed that this little devil was a woman?

Looking around, I realized that somehow I was in two places at once—Leslie's room and in the temple of Kailas.

"Is it possible that there is a grain of truth in what I have just been thinking?" I asked the Devil.

"Much more than you think," he replied. "It is not simply a metaphor that the devil loves him like a woman. You have guessed what may possibly be the most important aspect of our relationship with you. I've already mentioned that it is very difficult for me to explain in full the essence and characteristics of the relationships of devils with people. There are things which you have to work out for yourself.

"Basically, we have no sex, but as we represent the reverse aspect of you, your sex is always reflected in us, but becomes the opposite. Do you understand? This little devil is not a woman. But in relation to Leslie, womanly traits appear in him, because Leslie is a man. Had Leslie been a woman, masculine traits would have appeared in the little devil."

"Does this mean that each one of us has such a 'she'," I asked, "and every woman has such a 'he'?"

"Not necessarily, but it is quite possible," replied the Devil. "Now you understand why the story of Adam and Eve and their 'love' disturbed us so much." The Devil sneered with contempt. "We were jealous of them. Some of

us were jealous of Adam because of Eve, others of Eve because of Adam, and some—like myself—who feel equally
male and female, were jealous in both directions at once.
You can understand it now, but had I told you everything at
once, you would not have understood a thing. In our relations with people, sex plays a large part; moreover, most
people are much more easily influenced when it is em-
ployed."

"Somehow I completely fail to understand you," I said.
"Earlier you said that you cannot see people experiencing
emotions of love. And now you say that the easiest way for
you to influence people is from that direction. Which is the
truth?"

"Both," said the Devil, not in the least put out. "The
emotions of sex disgust and alienate us when they give rise
to so-called romantic moods in people. Herein lies the main
evil. We spare no strength to fight it, but we can do nothing. These romantic moods surround a person like a wall
and we lose him completely until the romance is over.
Worse still, of course, is the connection of sex with the
mystical: that much-talked-about sense of the miraculous,
and feelings of immortality. These sensations take people
completely away from us and make them inaccessible to
our influence. On the other hand, the same emotion of sex
can be beneficent from our point of view: when it is connected with even the slightest feeling of aversion, with a
sense of guilt and shame, with furtiveness and a sense of
wrongdoing, that is just what we need. You see, the same
emotion in one man can manifest itself differently in others.
It can be for us or against us. It is only those who have the
capacity for romance or romantic moods, or who experience
'wonder' in the sensation of sex [the Devil pronounced
these words with scarcely disguised irritation], who are completely inaccessible to us. But fortunately this happens very

rarely. The majority of people, men and women, regard such things very realistically, without any romantic ideas. And it is very easy for us to deal with such people. This Leslie White was one of the difficult ones. However, he is an Englishman, and there is therefore so much prejudice and hypocrisy surrounding his attitude to sex that it is surely possible to find some line of attack. There is much that he fears in himself, much he does not believe. He feels guilty at the same time, and to justify himself in his own eyes, he tries to reduce all this to the lowest material level. It is there that we take him. And besides all this, you remember what I told you about 'play'? So long as people believe that in the experience of sex the realm of fact is not real, that the real is something else, they are inaccessible to us. But as soon as they begin to take it all seriously, and as a result of this become afraid and jealous, begin to hate and suffer, they are ours. You see there are emotions of a material order through which people become accessible to us. These emotions are effected most easily through sex."

I turned my eyes again to Leslie's room. The boy had brought some more whisky and soda, and Leslie was already cutting and turning the pages of a third book. The little devil, apparently, had despaired of finding him, and sat in the corner, totally dejected, obviously desperately anxious to think of a solution. Then he lay down on the floor, spread himself out like a frog until he became flat as a sheet of paper and, working his way along with his hands and feet, crawled under the door.

I became interested in where he would go now. Getting up from the floor, the little devil shook himself, swelled up like a balloon, and ran down the stairs. I began to watch him, leaving Leslie for the time being. The little devil came out through a locked door at the seashore and, waddling from side to side, he started walking along the sand. A dark wave was running up, leaving behind a line of white foam. The night was warm and dark, almost velvety. The stars were shining, and between the palm trees, like shooting stars, the fireflies were flitting. But the little devil did not pay attention to any of this, for at that moment he suddenly had the look of a rag-and-bone man, some petty hawker considering a cheap deal on the seashore under the palms. What business had he with these palm trees? They could not be cut and sold, and as for the fireflies, they had no market value. If you told a schemer like this that the night was enchanting and beautiful, it would seem nonsense to him. More probably, he would start thinking how he could knock a rupee or two out of this fool by selling him an artificial pearl, or something like that. The little devil seemed exactly such a cheapjack. He represented the impossibility of becoming aware of anything which holds enchantment or beauty. At this moment, I understood that our gravest mistake is in ascribing to the devil positive evil forces, such as demonic traits. There is nothing positive in the devil, nor can there be. This I saw quite clearly. The devil is the absence of all that is highest and most refined in human beings: absence of religious feeling, absence of vision, absence of the feeling for beauty, absence of awareness of the miraculous.

Swaying from side to side, the little devil walked fairly quickly over the sand beneath the palm trees, staring the whole time into the darkness, as if he were looking for something. Finally he turned aside, and I noticed that on the sand another devil sat by the thick trunk of a palm. By the look of him, he was fairly important. He had a fat belly, a gray goatee beard, and a skullcap. The little devil sat down on the sand opposite him and began apparently to tell him all about his failure with Leslie, pointing from time to time in the direction of the hotel. I could not make out what he was saying. I was struck, however, by how much he actually resembled a woman, as if he had combined in himself every objectionable and unpleasing feature found in a common and vulgar female. The old devil listened intently, then he began to speak, in obviously didactic tones. And the little devil sat in front of him, his head bent to one side, his chin on his palm, listening intently as if afraid to miss a word.

I returned to Leslie. He continued to read for a long time, writing down any thoughts which occurred to him. Later, he went to bed.

The night flashed quickly past me, and the short tropical dawn came. In India and in Ceylon one gets up early. The servants were sweeping the corridors, and carrying tea and coffee to the rooms. A Singhalese boy in a narrow white sarong and jacket, barefoot, and wearing a tortoise-shell comb on his head, silently entered Leslie's room with a big tray in his hands. Leslie was still asleep under the mosquito net. Treading lightly, the boy stopped and placed the tray on a low table by the bed.

I glanced at the tray and to my amazement I saw that everything on the tray was the devil, that same little devil I had left under the palm. Now the little devil assumed a diversity of forms, and, one must give him his due, he looked very attractive and appetizing. First, it was tea, two medium-sized dark teapots, one containing hot water, the other strong and fragrant Ceylon tea; amber-colored Australian butter with a piece of ice on a small plate, thick marmalade; a hot soft-boiled egg in a china eggcup; two pieces of cheese; a small heap of hot toast; four dark-yellow, curved bananas; two black-violet mangosteens, a fruit so tender that it cannot be brought to Europe. And all this was the little devil!

Leslie opened one eye and looked at the tray. Then he stretched and yawned, opened the other eye, and sat up in bed. I saw at once yesterday's thoughts come flooding back to him, and how cheerful he felt. How pleasant it was for him to remember it all: the talk with the Indian, his intention to study Yoga, and all the thoughts which had occurred to him in the evening.

"The whole point is in training. The old man is right," said Leslie to himself. "Above all, one must always observe oneself, not allow oneself to do anything without asking, Is this necessary for my aim?, and observe one's thoughts and words, and actions, so that everything is conscious."

I saw that Leslie found it enjoyable talking to himself like this and gratifying to think that he knew all about such things.

Soon he lifted the mosquito net and scrambled out. He was about to get up, but the tray, with the devil on it, caught his attention, and he involuntarily looked at the bananas.

I had guessed the trap set for him.

For a split second it seemed as if he were hesitating; but then in a businesslike manner he poured out a large cup of strong tea and spread a piece of toast thickly with marmalade.

Leslie was feeling exceptionally well. Everything in him longed to make a start, to work, and his conscience told him he could not deny himself a bit of pleasure.

Tea, toast, butter, marmalade, an egg, bananas, cheese— all disappeared very quickly. Making a slight cut with a knife, Leslie broke the thick black shell of the mangosteen and took out the tender white fruit; it looks like a mandarin, is faintly acid and aromatic, and melts in the mouth. A second one followed the first. And that was the end of it. Glancing at the tray with some regret, Leslie began to get up. While he was washing and shaving, the little devil appeared again by him. He had a crumpled look, but beyond all doubt he could see Leslie now.

Leslie was thinking about everything as before, only his thoughts were, so to speak, slightly duller. I could not now detect that aura of creativeness apparent in his thoughts the previous evening. The thoughts seemed to go around in the same circle. However, Leslie held them fast, and apparently they were welcome to him. Leslie finished dressing, came down, walked through the dining room, and went out on the verandah facing the sea. In front of the verandah there was a small lawn, and further on, beyond the palm trees, was the sea, blue and glittering. On the right, the green shore ran toward Colombo, and one could see the tops of the sails on the fishermen's catamarans drying where they had been dragged onto the sand. Leslie glanced involuntarily in that direction. True, he had come out here simply because the boy was tidying the room, and he intended to work until lunchtime. But right now the sea was drawing him. Here there was so much sun, and the light breeze, with the smell of water, caressed him. Leslie felt how good it would be to rock in the catamaran over the clear waves, and once again to think over yesterday's talk.

"No, it is better to work," he said to himself. "One must not start, right away, by giving in. I will go only to see that everything in the catamaran is in order."

Whistling, he ran down the stone steps built into the sea, and I saw that the little devil, just like a dog, dashed off ahead at full speed.

A young Singhalese fisherman, whom Leslie always took out to sea with him, was standing by the boats. He was listening very attentively to an old fisherman, trying not to miss a single word. The old man, whose gray hair was plaited at the back of his head, was telling him about his court case against a rich man called de Silva, whose car had killed a calf.

There is nothing in the world more interesting to the Singhalese and the Tamils in Ceylon, indeed in the whole of India up to the Himalayas, than a court case. Law courts are the most popular form of entertainment of the Indians, and the favorite theme of conversations. In the time of the rajahs there was no such justice, because right belonged to the one who paid the most. This did not afford any kind of interest, because it was known in advance who would pay more, and thus who would be in the right. But the English introduced real courts of law, in which it was never known in advance who would win. Such trials added an element of chance, and became a popular pastime. The people of India took enthusiastic advantage of this new entertainment. The court is theater, club, and circus; it is a snake-charming, a fistfight, and a cockfight, all at the same time and place. Legal experts enjoy immense respect and authority. And everyone is always at law, prosecuting somebody. Only the very poorest and most unfortunate person has no legal case. But then he is himself being sued for something or other.

The young fisherman was completely immersed in the elaborate evidence put forward by the owner of the killed calf. However, at that moment the little devil ran up to him, hit him on the shoulder with his fist, and pushed him in the direction of the hotel.

Seeing Leslie coming down to the sea, the boy assumed he was going out in his catamaran, and tearing himself away from the fascinating story with some regret, he rushed at once to meet Leslie with a radiant face.

"Master wants to go to sea. Wonderful weather, Master. There is not much wind, but we will put up the sails at once. Everything will be ready right now, Master."

Without waiting for an answer, the boy, his head low-

ered and naked heels flashing, raced off to Leslie's catamaran, which was beached some distance from the others.

Without intending to, Leslie caught his enthusiasm,
and smiling, followed him. As things have turned out, he
decided, it would do no harm to spend half an hour on the
sea.

Out at sea the wind was stronger than it had seemed
ashore. The catamaran rose and fell, gliding over the waves
like an iceboat on ice, responding to every movement of the
rudder. Leslie did not have the heart to turn back for a long
time. However, on the return trip, they had to beat against
the oncoming fresh wind, and as a result Leslie did not get
back to the hotel until half past nine.

Breakfast was nearly over when he walked through the
dining room. Although he felt pretty hungry after two
hours on the water, he wanted to go straight to his room
so as not to lose any more time. But the head boy, barefoot
in a narrow white sarong and white dinner jacket, with a
tortoise-shell comb on his head, bowed to him with such
deep respect, as only Indian servants know how, that Leslie
without thinking went up to his own table and sat down.

Overtaking him, the little devil had already jumped on
the table and turned into the menu, coquettishly leaning
against a vase of flowers.

The young boy brought tea and marmalade, as is customary at the first breakfast, and stood waiting for further
orders.

Leslie poured himself a large cup of strong tea, and
on taking a sip, glanced at the menu and ordered the
traditional English grilled smoked herring. After the herring, he asked for another national dish, fried eggs and
bacon, then a medium-sized steak with fried onions, then
an Indian dish, curry, which is served nowhere else as it is
in Ceylon. Serving curry is a ritual in itself. First of all, the

head boy brought in a large tureen of hot, fluffy, fragrant rice. Leslie put a large portion on his plate. Afterwards, another boy brought two dishes with casters full of different sauces—sauces made of crayfish necks, fish, eggs, and tomato, with chunks of meat, a repulsive yellow sauce of curry roots, and a sauce of some kind of lentil. Leslie helped himself from three serving dishes. Then a third boy brought a large dish, divided into about twelve sections; this held grated coconut and a small, dried, stinking fish, pepper in all sorts of guises, chopped onions, some very hot yellow paste, and various other strange condiments. And finally the head boy put before Leslie a bowl of hot mango chutney.

While Leslie was helping himself to the different ingredients of curry, and mixing them on his plate, as is the custom, I saw with horror that all this was the little devil. His feet stuck out of one tureen, his head bobbed about in another.

Following the curry, which made his mouth burn terribly, Leslie drank two more cups of tea and ate several pieces of toast and marmalade. Then he had some cheese, and, refusing sweets, began to eat fruit—an orange, several bananas, and then a mango. Mango is a fairly big, dark-green, heavy, and cold fruit. Holding it on a plate with the left hand, one cuts off large pieces around the kernel with a knife, and then eats the cold, aromatic, and succulent pulp with a spoon. It tastes like a mixture of pineapple and peach ice cream, sometimes with a hint of strawberries. Two mangos, a bottle of ginger, and a cigarette finished off Leslie White's breakfast.

Smoking a cigarette, Leslie remembered he had to go to town. This was annoying, because it meant again putting off his work.

The train ran beneath the palms along the seashore. A

green wave rose, lifted like a glass rampart, and fell, scattering white foam on the sand and rolling right up to the train.
The sea was so brilliant and glittering that one's eyes hurt
to look at it. But Leslie did not particularly want to
look at any of this. Just at present he felt that he saw it
all every day and it seemed to him that the train was going exceedingly slowly. He had to call in at work and at
the tailor's and then return for lunch. He had no desire to
think, but it was pleasant to remember that he had something very good in store, to which he would return when
the time came.

The little devil was here too, though he looked rather
tired (I realized that he did not achieve the two breakfasts
for Leslie White without a price). At the same time, he
was, apparently, very pleased with himself. He climbed onto
the seat opposite Leslie and sat, now and again looking
out of the window.

Leslie returned to his hotel at twenty past one. It was hot,
with the usual Ceylon hothouse heat. Leslie went to his
room to wash and change, and in a fresh white suit and an
immaculate soft collar, he came down to the dining room
Lunch was in progress. At a small table next to Leslie's sat
his regular neighbor, a retired Indian colonel. Before the
meal he had finished a bottle of stout with ice, which he
drank for health reasons, and now regarded the world with
a good-humored and benign gaze. Cheerfully Leslie greeted
the colonel and unrolled his table napkin.

The boy put a plate of tomato soup in front of him;
however, I saw that it was really that same little devil. After the soup the little devil became a soft-boiled turbot.
Then fried chicken with ham and green salad. Then cold
mutton with jam and jelly, then wildfowl paté, and then

again curry, which was served with the same pomp on twenty-five small plates. All this, Leslie conscientiously put away. After curry, the little devil turned into ice cream and then fruit—oranges, mango and pineapple.

Having finished the lunch, Leslie got up, feeling somewhat heavy.

"Well, now I will read at leisure," he told himself, "then I must get to Lady Gerald's for tea."

Leslie went to his room, ordered soda water and lemon, took off nearly everything he could, and sat down by the table with a book and pipe.

He read one page very attentively, but in the middle of the second page, he suddenly caught himself repeating a sentence without being able to understand what it meant. At the same time he felt a strange heaviness in the temples and when he looked around toward the bed, he noticed, as if for the first time, that it looked particularly attractive. Mechanically he put the book down, went over to the bed, and yawned. The little devil was already fidgeting about smoothing the pillowcase. Leslie glanced at his watch and lay down on the bed. He fell almost at once into a deep and healthy sleep. Meanwhile the little devil climbed into the armchair by the table, took Leslie's unfinished pipe and the book he had been reading, and, looking very self-important, began puffing clouds of smoke and turning the pages of the book, which he purposely held upside down.

Leslie slept for two hours so soundly that when he woke up he did not know at first whether it was morning or evening. Finally he looked at his watch and seeing that it was already half past four, he jumped out of bed and began to wash and dress. The boy again brought him soda water and lemon, and within fifteen minutes, looking fresh and neat, Leslie was running to the station next to the hotel. In front of him ran the little devil.

The five o'clock tea given by Lady Gerald was served in

the garden. I was astonished when I saw Leslie White at
one table with two ladies; one, a tall, slender blonde, was
Margaret Ingleby. Now I understood why Leslie was in
such a hurry.

I had met Margaret some two years before this in Venice, and I did not know that she had arrived in Ceylon. She
was here with her aunt, a rather talkative gray-haired lady,
and, as I understood from the conversation, Leslie was meeting her for the second time only. Now he was enthusiasti-
cally telling Margaret about Ceylon, and their conversation
was not at all like the small talk going on at the other
tables. Lady Gerald took the aunt away to show her some
Indian rarities and Margaret remained alone with Leslie. I
could not help seeing that they were very taken with each
other, and that Margaret was the first to admit it.

I had always liked her very much. She had the interesting style of a woman from an eighteenth-century painting
or engraving. "A woman to her fingertips," one French
artist said about her. Not a trace of the hardness or abrupt-
ness of movement usual with the Englishwomen who play
golf. She had a wonderfully chiseled neck, a small mouth—
also a great rarity in an Englishwoman—a particularly in
dividual shape to her lips, enormous gray eyes, a musical
voice, and a slow and slightly lazy manner of speaking.

She saw that she made an impression on Leslie, and
this pleased her, quite apart from any other considerations.
She knew that Leslie was entirely out of the question for
her. The aunt, with her usual garrulousness, had already
spoken about him to Lady Gerald, and Margaret had heard
that Leslie had no money, lived on a salary, was twenty-
eight years old, and that even under the most favorable circumstances would not be able to marry for ten years. Margaret was already twenty-nine herself, and she had decided
that she would be married within a year at the very latest.
In the last resort she would take one of her ever-faithful

admirers, of whom there were three. This did not diminish her interest, however, and she felt attracted to Leslie. He was not like the others, he spoke fascinatingly of things which interested her and which nobody else knew about. It pleased her to sit here in the wicker chair listening to Leslie and watching how his eyes from time to time, involuntarily, glanced over her legs and how suddenly, by an effort of will, he raised them again.

Observing them, I suddenly noticed something familiar and, looking more closely, I saw that Leslie and Margaret were Adam and Eve.

But, oh Lord, how many obstacles had now been piled up between them! I understood what was meant by the angel with the fiery sword. They could not even look at each other without uneasiness. At the same time they both felt that they knew each other well, and had known each other for a long time, and if they had allowed themselves the liberty they could have entered at once into a much closer intimacy. But they knew very well that they would not permit themselves the liberty, even though it was strange and almost ridiculous how close they were to each other.

They were finishing tea, and Leslie, before whom the little devil had pushed a plate of sandwiches from behind his left elbow, mechanically demolished a fair-sized heap.

"Let us go and look at your sea," Margaret said in her slow and melodious voice. Leslie got up, feeling slightly alarmed lest somebody should approach them. Luckily, nobody joined them. Many were leaving. In the corner of the garden was a stone summerhouse with branches and steps to the beach. Here they sat down, and Leslie placed himself so as to see in front of him Margaret's silhouette against the background of sea and sky. To the right of them, the large red sphere of the sun was descending low over the dark-blue horizon of the sea. The waves were lapping gently, and there was a breath of wind as the pre-dusk silence settled over the whole of nature.

Leslie was speaking about yesterday's discussion with the Indian.

"What surprised me most were my own feelings," Leslie was saying. "I am not in the least sentimental, and yet, at the time of the conversation, I felt a positively tender feeling toward this old man, as if he were my father, whom I had not seen for years, whom I had lost and suddenly found. It was something like that. You understand? Actually, I did not agree with much of what he was saying. This feeling went somehow counter to my consciousness."

"So it means that India really exists," Margaret was saying. "No, you simply must get to know everything completely. Just think how fascinating it all is. Suddenly you will find a real miracle. I have read everything that has been written about it, but the most important things are usually left out. And you feel that the people who write the books know nothing themselves and take anybody's word for it."

Leslie listened to Margaret with admiration. She literally spoke his thoughts, and in his own words.

"No, this old man made quite a different impression," he said. "I felt, without any doubt, that he knew and that through him it was possible to find people who know still more . . ."

Suddenly, Leslie felt that everything he was saying about the Indian acquired some special new meaning because he was saying it to Margaret. Leslie suddenly understood that if he could take the two steps which separated him from Margaret and then take her by the waist and lead her right down to the sea, walk with her along the water's edge, feel it roll under their feet, further and further on, until the stars began to shine, somewhere where there were no people but only the two of them, then, straight away, everything which the old Indian had spoken about would become a complete reality. And he would not need any kind of Yoga, nor any kind of study, he would only need to go with Margaret along the seashore, to look at the stars, to wait for the sun to rise, to rest in a forest thicket during the midday heat, and in the evening to go out again to the sea and to walk, and walk always further and further on . . .

At the same moment Leslie felt suddenly how well and how intimately he knew Margaret. He knew the touch of her hands and of her entire body, the smell of her hair, the look of her eyes quite close to his own, the light movement of her lashes, the touch of her cheek, her lips, the feeling of her moving body . . . and all this passed suddenly, like a dream. For a brief split second, he remembered Margaret and remembered an evening exactly like this on exactly the same seashore. In the same way the red sphere of the sun had sunk into the darkening sea, in the same way the surf could be heard running up, in the same way had the palm trees rustled . . .

The experience was so strong that it took his breath away, and he suddenly fell silent.

Margaret listened to him, leaning slightly toward him. Everything he said was new and interesting. But it amused her, for what she wanted was something quite different. She laughed inwardly at the thought of how astonished Leslie White would be if she had done what she was thinking of. She would have liked to take Leslie by the shoulders, just like a young girl, and shake him. Instinctively, she felt how strong and heavy he was, and could feel his firm but at the same time supple and flexible body. She felt that if she did take Leslie by the shoulders, she would not be able to move him. Her awareness of this strength and this living weight was somehow particularly pleasant. It blended with her awareness of his gaze, which she could feel returning again and again to her ankles, her hands, and her lips every time he had made the effort to look away.

"You silly," she was saying to herself, "if you could only know what I am thinking." Her eyes began to sparkle with fire.

"Where is the little devil?" I thought. "It would be interesting to know what he is doing now. Is it possible that Leslie has eaten him up completely?"

But at that moment, I saw the head of the little devil projecting from under the bench on which Leslie sat, with his gaze fixed firmly on Margaret.

Even I was startled. Here was the very green-eyed monster itself. It was here that the satanic nature of the devil revealed itself in its entirety. There was infinite hatred and malice in his look, and a kind of coarse repulsive cynicism and madness. Apparently, what was tearing at the devil's very vitals was fear.

"What is he afraid of?" I asked the Devil.

"Can you really not understand?" he replied. "Leslie might disappear from him at any moment. But think what he must feel. To have this happen, after all his self-sacrifice! You saw how he loves Leslie. And now because of this wretched girl all his labors may be in vain. You can see that Leslie is again absorbed in these fantasies. And now they are particularly dangerous. You have noticed that he already remembers; of course, he cannot understand these memories, but all the same he is very near to dangerous discoveries."

"You say that he can disappear. How?" I asked.

"If he takes the one step," said the Devil.

"What step?"

"The one step which is separating them. Only he will not do it. Just think, in Lady Gerald's garden! Of course not! What can he do? As it is, they have been sitting too long by themselves. This can only be excused by Margaret's recent arrival and by saying that things like the setting sun from the seashore fascinate her."

Actually they had not been sitting together very long, not even as long as it takes me to tell this tale. I realized this because the sun, which had been touching the horizon with a golden edge when they came out onto the beach was sending out its last rays and had not yet set completely. And the sun sets very quickly.

However, Margaret had already noticed the strangeness of the situation and with a little effort tore herself from the realm of fancy which had begun to carry her away.

She noticed how Leslie's voice had changed, how suddenly he had fallen silent. She felt that she must save the situation or something silly would happen. She had nothing to fear. What could one fear in Lady Gerald's garden? The Devil was quite right. Margaret was almost certain that Leslie would not say anything. But even the silence became too significant.

Margaret began to talk, therefore, giving her voice a slightly mocking metallic inflection which she knew from experience acted very well on men and had helped her out of many a difficult situation in life.

As far back as her schooldays she had been given the name of "icy Margaret."

"I wonder what has become of Lady Gerald's guests," she said. "It seems we are alone on a desert island."

Three full seconds passed before Leslie found his voice and answered. But when he started to speak, Margaret knew that the crisis had passed.

"Probably they went to the sea," Leslie said, getting up.

Margaret ran down the stone steps and they saw not far away a group of men and women near the coconut trees. The Singhalese boys were demonstrating their skill, and there were ten of them, up one palm tree, climbing together just like monkeys.

Leslie and Margaret went in that direction. But now Margaret began rather to regret the mood she had frightened away. She, too, vaguely remembered something, but her memories were different. She felt as if she were a little girl and Leslie a small boy. She wanted to pull him by the sleeve, throw a handful of sand at him and run off, shouting at him to catch her.

"How boring it is to be grown up, how nice it would have been to play games with him," Margaret had time to tell herself.

They were already approaching a group of Lady Gerald's guests. All were laughing and talking. A tall German in a glaring yellow linen suit (sold in Port Said especially for German travelers) was clicking away with his Kodak, taking snapshots of the climbing boys.

"It is too dark," Margaret said softly, "or can one still take photographs?" she asked, turning to Leslie. She felt herself at fault with him, and she wanted to redress the wrong.

"It depends on the kind of camera," said Leslie. "Do you take photographs?"

"Yes, and I have a very good and expensive camera," said Margaret, and remembered in passing one of her faithful admirers who had given it to her, "only I do not know how to use it."

"It is possible with a good camera," said Leslie, still feeling resentful. "If you stand with your back to the sea, with the lens set at $f/4.5$, you can now take photographs at one-hundredth of a second on the most sensitive plate, and one-fiftieth on film. But nothing will come out for that character with the Brownie," he added, softening and feeling that he could not be angry with Margaret for long.

"But just look at that yellow suit and the sky-blue tie.

That is a German tourist's notion of a tropical outfit. I wonder where Lady Gerald catches such characters."

Glancing at Margaret as he spoke, he suddenly felt a sadness so agonizing that he was amazed. It was as though he remembered something in the distant past, of losing Margaret in exactly the same way as he was about to lose her now. At once everything became dull and disgusting, the whole world turned into a German in a fool's costume with a fool's accent.

Two ladies began to talk to Margaret. Leslie moved away and began to smoke. If he could have seen the little devil, he would have noticed that the devil first followed Margaret with his eyes full of spite and triumph, then turned three somersaults on the sand, ran up to Leslie, and stood opposite him, mimicking his movements and pretending to smoke a twig.

Later they all went to the house and said goodbye to each other. When Leslie took Margaret's warm soft hand, an electric current passed between them. This was the last time.

Afterwards Leslie returned home by the same railway. He sat alone in the compartment, smoking a pipe, and in his soul there was a whirlwind of the most contradictory thoughts and moods.

On the one hand, all his thoughts about seeking the miraculous took on a new, completely different aspect when the thought of Margaret mingled with them. On the other hand, he knew that he could not even dream of Margaret.

He had long ago come to the conclusion that because of his habits and his views it was necessary for him to remain single. And now he felt he must hold on to this thought, and allow himself no hesitation nor digression from it. He had no money to speak of. The Service he could tolerate only so long as he knew that he could give it up at any time. Dreaming of love would be a weakness, nothing more, Margaret must marry, maybe she was already engaged. Lady Gerald would know. Anyway—could he think of marriage? Married, he'd be bound, tethered to one place, to the Service. He would have to make thousands of concessions and compromises the whole time which he would never agree to now. And besides, anyway, it was impossible. His salary was just enough for him alone. One cannot live with a wife in a hotel. In order to marry he would need five times more than he was earning now.

Leslie talked these sensible notions over with himself. At the same time, he felt that in Margaret there was something sweeping aside all prudence and logic, something for the sake of which one could begin everything again, agree to everything and not think about it.

"Yes, Margaret . . ." he said to himself, as if this name were a magic invocation making everything impossible possible.

The little devil who was lying on the seat rolled up in a ball, growled like a dog, and opening one eye glared at Leslie with undisguised hatred.

"No, I must not think of it," Leslie said to himself.

He closed his eyes resolutely, settled back on the seat, and tried to visualize the face of the old Indian, wanting to recall the memory of his words. Instead, he saw Margaret saying slowly: "Let us go and look at your sea."

"Darling," Leslie said silently, and the little devil gnashed his teeth and shriveled into a lump. Apparently he was not feeling well, because at times he shivered like a stray dog in the rain.

Leslie was absorbed in reveries, vague but unusually pleasant, daydreams in which Margaret became entangled with strange wonders, and about the Yogis Leslie was to find, with the help of the old Indian, in certain secret caves.

"There must be something in all this," he said to himself. "That Russian [which was myself] is quite right we must find new forces. With what we have already, we cannot organize our lives, we can only lose. We must find some new key to life, then everything will be possible."

The whole time, vague but tantalizingly delightful pictures flashed through Leslie's mind, in which the central figure was always Margaret.

As usually happens in such cases, his consciousness divided in two. One Leslie knew perfectly well that within the limits of ordinary earthly possibilities, Margaret was as inaccessible to him as a dweller on the moon. But the other Leslie did not at all want to take into consideration any of the earthly possibilities, for he was already building something fantastic and rearranging the bricks of life according to his own ideas.

It was exceptionally delightful to think of Margaret. Permitting himself these reveries, these dreams about Margaret unbeknownst to her, made Leslie feel like the knight who serves his princess even without her being aware of it. When he had achieved something, when he had found something, he would write and tell her what an impression their meeting had made on him, how much Margaret had done for him without herself suspecting it, how he was searching for her and found the "miraculous."

As soon as Leslie came to a break in his reveries, another voice in him at once picked up the thread and went on to say that "Margaret could answer his letter, could write that she often remembered Ceylon, remembered their meeting and conversation and wanted to come again, if not this year, the next."

Leslie was daydreaming just like a schoolboy, but in these dreams there was more reality than he himself could ever suspect. To many it would appear simply absurd to waste any time on such castles in the air, but I long ago became accustomed to the idea that the most fantastic things in life are the most real. I knew Margaret well, because I knew her type, and Leslie's dreams did not strike me as at all impossible. In fact, it is just such dreams which have the chance to come true. Margaret considered herself to be very positive and practical. However, she was mistaken. In fact, she was one of those women who are born under a special combination of planets, thanks to which they are accessible to influences of the fantastic and the miraculous. Should Leslie ever be able to touch upon these strings of her soul, she would follow him, without asking for anything else.

The little devil was apparently of the same opinion as I, because he was greatly displeased with Leslie's dreams. He woke up and sat making grimaces, as if he had a toothache. And then, apparently unable to stand any more, he leaped up and jumped out of the window.

Turning three somersaults in the air, the little devil flew into the window of a narrow third-class compartment, where it was completely dark (third-class coaches are not lit in Ceylon), very crowded and noisy. There he interfered in a quarrel which had just begun, and in a short time brought it to a fairly lively state. This slightly improved his mood, and when he caught up with Leslie on the way from the station to the hotel, he was not looking as wretched as before; you could see that he was ready for a further struggle. I did notice, however, that usually toward evening he became only the shadow of himself, so difficult was it to keep watch over Leslie White.

Leslie went to his room and, without putting on the light, sat down by the table. In this room reality at once rushed at him and he became very clearly aware that he would not see Margaret any more. Tomorrow morning she was leaving for Kandy and going on from there to India. His leave was ending shortly, and most likely he would be sent on a mission to the jungle in the southwestern part of the island.

He got up and switched on the light. His eyes squinting because of its brightness, he closed the shutters and took out of the table drawer a thick copy-book, in which he had taken notes yesterday.

How strangely foreign everything which he had been writing yesterday seemed to him today. As if a year had passed since yesterday evening. Everything was so naive, almost childish. Leslie recalled the morning and sailing in the catamaran. This also was long ago. Now suddenly he began to understand much that was new, as though his eyes had been opened. All this had happened during the course of the last two hours—from the talk with Margaret, from sensations that overwhelmed him, from dim memories of something other. All yesterday's thoughts had somehow reconstructed themselves in a new way, since Margaret had entered them, and now they became much nearer, much more real, and at the same time even more inaccessible, more difficult.

"Must sort all this out," Leslie told himself and involuntarily looked around. For some reason, at that moment, the hotel room appeared especially empty and dull to him.

Somebody knocked at the door.

"Come to dinner, White," said a voice outside the door. "A man has arrived, a mineralogist from Patnapuri; you must come and meet him."

Leslie did not want to go to dinner, but the four walls looked very inhospitable. It seemed too gloomy to sit here alone. He was quite glad to have an excuse to leave and seek some company.

"All right," he said.

For another half-second Leslie wavered. It was tedious to dress. But at the same time he felt that he could not sit through the whole evening alone. He had heard before about this mineralogist from Patnapuri as a person who was in love with Ceylon, knowing local life better than natives of the island. He was the sort of man Leslie liked to meet, because one could always learn something new from him.

Leslie got up reluctantly and began to undress. The little devil simply whizzed around him. Soon, dressed in a dinner jacket, a high collar, and patent-leather shoes, Leslie was on his way to the dining room.

"Hello, White, come over here," called the company at the bar. He was introduced to the mineralogist, and at the same time, the little devil bounded into a large goblet of whisky which ended up in Leslie's hand. Very puzzled, Leslie looked at the wine glass, but he drank it. "No, thank you," he said when he was offered another—he did not want to drink. However, the mineralogist interested him. He was a small man, black as a beetle, who won him over immediately with Singhalese anecdotes.

The whole company went to the dining room. The little devil raced ahead and changed into a bowl of turtle soup which was placed in front of Leslie. The colonel was dining in town, and in his place sat the mineralogist. During the conversation Leslie finished the soup, and ordered a bottle of wine in honor of the guest. The little devil took advantage of this and changed into crab mayonnaise. It looked very appetizing, and Leslie took more than common sense dictated. Iced white wine dispelled the feeling that there had been too much of the mayonnaise. The little devil, however, had by now turned into a fried fish with a subtle sauce. When Leslie was finishing his portion, I noticed that the little devil, staggering and holding his head, went away from the table.

Turtle steak was served, then fried duck with salad. All this, of course, was the little devil. Although it did not come easily to the little devil, he nevertheless decided to deal the final blow to Leslie, while Leslie, who never had any trouble with his stomach, ate everything that was put in front of him—more than usual in fact, because he felt disappointed with life when he remembered Margaret.

The little devil changed into roast lamb with a piquant sauce. Then into turkey, fried with ham, then pudding, then sweet cream; then, goodness knows why, after the sweet, hot toast and caviar. The usual absurd Ceylonese menu was spread on the table—some fifteen rather badly prepared dishes, all for some reason tasting alike, but with a great variety of sharp condiments, more suitable for the North Pole than the equator.

After all this, with the last of his strength, the little devil changed into almonds, blue raisins, and a very sharp and hot Indian dessert of sugared fruit with ginger, and at the end stood in front of Leslie as a small cup of coffee. Although Leslie was a very healthy person, even he became aware of the heaviness throughout his body.

The mineralogist was going to town. Leslie's two other neighbors were going to play bridge nearby. He remained alone. "Well, that is excellent," he thought lazily. "I will go and work."

He got up, but after a moment's hesitation, he went not to his room but out on the verandah. "Must drink some soda," he said to himself. "Large whisky and soda," he said to the boy.

On the glass-covered verandah, in low reclining armchairs, four people dozed with evening papers. Leslie filled his pipe and took a paper. The whisky was brought. He took a sip from the glass, smoked lazily for a while, and yawned.

There was something he had to think over, but the thoughts only crawled lazily through his mind.

"Tomorrow I will contemplate it all," said Leslie to himself.

After half a minute he put his pipe, which had gone out, on the table. Then he turned his head to one side and sighed deeply; within another half a minute his breathing had become regular.

Leslie was asleep.

But on the arm of the armchair, still not wanting to leave him, hung the little devil, completely transparent and soft, like a deflated balloon.

"You see," said the Devil, "that is what our life is like. Is that not self-sacrifice? Think of it, the poor little devil must keep watch over every step he takes, not leaving him even for one moment. He allows himself to be eaten up, works himself into such a state, and there is still the risk of losing him because of various silly fantasies. Tell me, is there anyone among you who would be capable of doing something like that? What would happen to you without us?"

"I won't argue," I said. "I see that you put a lot of effort and ingenuity into holding us in your hands. But I do not believe that such simple methods will work for long."

"They have been working ever since the time of Adam," the Devil said modestly. "Their main merit is that they are simple and do not arouse any suspicion.

"People fall into two categories on this matter. Some do not suspect danger from our side—even when it is pointed out to them, they refuse to recognize it. You see, it makes them laugh to think that breakfasts, lunches, and

dinners can have some bearing on their 'spiritual development' and can obstruct it or prevent it. The very thought
of such dependence of the spirit on the body seems offen-
sive to them. They cannot tolerate it, out of false pride, and
do not want to take it into consideration. In their opinion,
one side of life goes on quite independently from the other.
Of course, as a result of this, everyone who deludes himself
like this is ours already.

"On the other hand, people with a bit of brain will understand where the danger lies, but at once go to the other
extreme. They begin to preach abstinence and asceticism,
and to claim that this is good in itself, pleasing to God, and
of a higher morality. Along with this, as usual, they do not
watch themselves so much as their own neighbors. These
are our favorite helpers."

"All the same, I am convinced that Leslie White will
reach the essence of the matter, now that he has become
interested in Yoga."

The Devil, quite obviously furious, stamped with his
hoof, and a shower of sparks flew from the stone.

"You are right this time," he said. "Leslie has reached
the essence of the matter, and what is even worse, he has
found ways of communication with other such lunatics.
This creates a very dangerous situation for him.

"It started as follows: while traveling to the south of
Ceylon, he revisited that Buddhist monastery where you
met him. Well, you know how he likes to poke his nose
into everything. Inquiring into the life of the monks, he
became very interested in knowing what they ate, how they
ate, and when they ate. And when he was told that they
eat nothing after midday, according to the rules for Buddhist monks, he was most eager to know why it was so.

"In the end he decided to try such a regimen for himself, and now he lives on rice and fruit and eats once a day.

He is playing a dangerous game. But there is something still worse. The thought occurred to him that he was not alone. You know when this thought occurs to a person, he will very quickly find confirmation. In the end, he learned about the existence of a chain. To put it another way, it all happened just as the old Indian had promised. Out of the dark night he saw the lights of people going to the one temple, to the same feast. Well, that was bad enough. I do not believe in this gibberish. But it is very dangerous for people, particularly such types as Leslie White who are not satisfied with fine words and good intentions. I do not know what kind of feast it is. All those people go to their own destruction; they are flying, like butterflies into the fire. I have told you all this before.

"You see, one has to put up occasionally with their self-destruction, although one pities them. The trouble is that they drag others after them. That is terrible. I do not believe in a mystical chain, nor in a temple, but I must tell you that the awakening of tendencies in this direction frightens me. In the end I will have to resort to special methods, also fairly old, and I will have to apply them in greater measure."

"What are these methods?" I asked.

"That I cannot tell you now. As it is, I have given away too much. I will say only that 'the stake is on nobility,' and in this game I have never once lost."

"Frankly, I have been astonished that you have trusted me with such confidences," I said. "You know, I can tell all this to people."

The Devil laughed with a horrid rattling laugh.

"You can talk as much as you like," he said. "Nobody will believe you. The descendants of the animals will not believe you, because there is no profit in it for them, and the descendants of Adam will not believe you, out of gen-

erosity—they decided, at all costs, to consider the descendants of the animals to be equal with them or even to
consider themselves to be descendants of the animals. And
besides, I have a special way of preventing any such talk
for a long time. Now, farewell!"

Evidently the Devil wanted to give me a surprise when
he left. He suddenly began to rise and grow taller. Soon he
became taller than the elephant, then grew larger than the
pagodas. And, finally he became a huge black shadow, in
front of which I felt shrunk to a pinpoint, as has happened
sometimes in the mountains.

The Black Shadow began to move, I followed it. On
the plain, the Shadow became even bigger, rising up to the
sky. Then, at its back two black wings stretched out, and it
began to separate from the earth, gradually spreading out
all over the sky like a black cloud.

With this image in my mind, I woke up.

The rain was coming down in torrents. The sky was
covered with gray clouds, and along the slopes of the mountains, moving scraps of mist were scattered, thickening in
each hollow. I felt tired, broken, and ill. Having stood for
a while on the verandah, I decided not to go anywhere, that
I did not want to see anything and I would go back. To
reach the temples in this rain was impossible anyway, and
now by day the caves no longer interested me. I felt that
they would be empty.

While my driver was harnessing the horses to the tonga,
I hastily collected my things, as for some reason I wanted
to leave as soon as possible. I gave little thought to my
dream. I could not even tell whether it had really been a
dream, or I had just imagined it, because of the tedium of
sleeplessness . . .

Later we traveled again from one mountain to another, past precipices where far below black ruins loomed, the remains of water mains and drains; we passed the gates of dead walled towns, whose houses had trees growing inside them; past Daulatabad, with its fortress on a round rock which Pierre Loti, an occasional visitor here, said was like an unfinished tower of Babylon, its minaret now inhabited by wild bees.

At the station I heard the bad news that the railway tracks had been washed away and that I would have to wait goodness knows how long until they were repaired. As a result I was stranded for three days. But that is just one of the delights of traveling in India, during the rainy season.

Before long I left India, and on the way to Europe, the news of war overtook me.

In October, in London, I saw Leslie White once more.

I was riding on top of a bus from the Strand to Piccadilly, and at the corner of Haymarket we were stopped by passing soldiers.

The bagpipes were gaily playing a lively march to the loud roll of drums, and in front of us passed what appeared to be a newly formed Scottish regiment. In front, on a tall English thoroughbred, a colonel was riding upright and broad-shouldered, with a large, drooping mustache and a small beribboned cap. Following him were rows of soldiers intermingled with volunteers, many of whom were without uniforms; some still wearing coats but with Scottish caps, others even hats, but all carrying rifles, all strong, tall, and walking with that long light stride peculiar to the marching of Scottish regiments. They were astonishingly stylish, I simply could not take my eyes off them, the colonel on his horse, and the tall, lean, noncommissioned officer with bare knees who was passing on my side— –in all of them was something which makes the Scots distinct from soldiers anywhere else.

In my opinion, this peculiarity they have inherited from Rome. Scottish soldiers are Roman soldiers: they have retained their stride, their type, and their costume. The bare-kneed uniform of the Scots which we think very amusing, saying that they are dressed in "skirts," is in fact the Roman costume surviving two thousand years. Now the stern simplicity of khaki, replacing the traditional Scottish tartan, has brought them still closer to Rome.

These thoughts and many others, tormenting and contrary thoughts about the war I had lived with for two months, flashed through my mind while I was looking at the soldiers. I was again aware of the whole of that nightmare from which, at times, I still hoped to wake up.

One platoon spread out and got out of step. The tall lieutenant, who was marching alongside, turned and tersely gave a command. The young soldiers, laughing, ran up, evened out, and quickly caught up with the beat of the march. The lieutenant stopped, a serious expression on his face as the men filed past him. It was Leslie White.

The pipes played gaily and the drums rolled, the soldiers and volunteers passed cheerfully by with short rifles on their shoulders. And I suddenly felt physically cold.

I could no longer look at the soldiers from an aesthetic standpoint, admiring their style.

I remembered everything: the caves of Ellora, the temple of Kailas, the black shadow of the Devil, and his threat which I had not then understood.

Now I knew that this was the special method which he intended to set in motion to distract Leslie White and others like him from harmful thoughts and ambitions. And I comprehended the incredible hopelessness of the situation.

On the one hand, the sacrifice of Leslie White and the others passing below was heroic. Had they and many others not decided to give up their life, youth, and freedom, the descendants of the animals would by now be quite openly ruling the world. Barbarians would long since have been in Paris, and perhaps by now they might have destroyed Notre Dame, as they have already ravaged the cathedral in Rheims. The wise old gargoyles which revealed so much to me would have perished, and this strange, complicated soul would have fled from the earth . . . How much more could they have destroyed . . . !

At the same time there was something still more terrible in all that was happening. I could see that the descendants of Adam might find themselves in different camps. What chance had they now of recognizing each other? Whether there was a chain or not, whether it had begun to come into being or not, I did not know. However, I felt that now the possibility for any kind of mutual understanding had been shattered for some time ahead. All the chessmen on the board of life were muddled up again. And from out of remote subterranean regions, banalities and vulgarities were being released into the world, together with clouds composed of lies and hypocrisy which people were being forced to breathe; how long this will continue I do not know.

The soldiers passed, and the heavy bus, swaying a little, set off again, overtaking the one in front.

"What has Leslie retained from Yoga, from Buddhism?" I asked myself. Now he must think, feel, and live like a Roman legionnaire, whose duty is to defend the Eternal City from the barbarians. An entirely different world, another psychology. Now all these refinements of thought seem an unnecessary luxury. Probably he has already forgotten about them or will soon forget. Who

in the end knows whether there are more barbarians outside the walls or within them? How does one recognize
them? The key, once again, has been thrown into the
deep sea.

"The stake is on nobility," I remembered the words of
the Devil. And had to admit that this time he had won.

A NOTE ON THE AUTHOR

Peter Demianovich Ouspensky was born in Moscow in 1878. At the University of Moscow he studied natural science and psychology, and his first book, *The Fourth Dimension,* earned him immediate respect as a mathematical theorist. However, he decided to become a journalist and writer, contributing to the principal Russian papers, writing books, and traveling widely between 1908 and 1915. The Revolution drove him from his home in St. Petersburg to the safety of Constantinople, where friends discovered him living in poverty. Lady Rothermere came across the American edition of his second book, *Tertium Organum,* and through her intervention he was able to come to England.

His life had been changed in 1915 by his meeting with the Caucasian teacher G. I. Gurdjieff, whose disciple he became. He was to set up, at Lyne Place near London, a self-supporting community which flourished for many years. Among the men and women who studied with Ouspensky there were J. D. Beresford, Algernon Blackwood, A. R. Orage, Christopher Isherwood, and Aldous Huxley. In 1940 he settled in America and formed a colony patterned after the institute. He died at Lyne Place in 1947.

Ouspensky's reputation rests mainly on *Tertium Organum,* the theme of which is the need to go beyond logical thinking to understand the nature of the real world. Western readers know Ouspensky largely through this book and through *In Search of the Miraculous,* which has become recognized as the most authoritative summary of Gurdjieff's ideas. Between these came *A New Model of the Universe,* based largely on his travels. *Talks with a Devil* was written about the same time, during a period of searching before Ouspensky met Gurdjieff. Originally published in Petrograd in 1916, this is the first translation of two stories extraordinarily relevant to our time.

A NOTE ON THE EDITOR

John G. Bennett is many things: mathematical physicist, linguist, lecturer, and author of many books, among them *The Crisis in Human Affairs, The Dramatic Universe* (4 vols.), and his new book, *Gurdjieff: The Making of a New World*. Born in 1897, for half a century he has been working actively to pass on to others the ideas of Gurdjieff and Ouspensky. He is now Principal of the International Academy for Continuous Education at Sherborne, Gloucestershire.

A NOTE ON THE TYPE

The text of this book was set on the Linotype in Garamond
No. 3, a modern rendering of the type first cut by Claude
Garamond (1510–1561). Garamond was a pupil of Geof-
frey Troy and is believed to have based his letters on the
Venetian models, although he introduced a number of
important differences, and it is to him we owe the letter
which we know as old-style. He gave to his letters a certain
elegance and a feeling of movement that won for their
creator an immediate reputation and the patronage of
Francis I of France.

Composed, printed, and bound by
American Book–Stratford Press, Inc.
New York, New York

Typography and binding design by
Virginia Tan